Also by the author:

NOVELS
Pushing the Bear
The Only Piece of Furniture
in the House

SHORT STORIES
Monkey Secret
Firesticks
Trigger Dance

ESSAYS
The West Pole
Claiming Breath

POETRY
Boom Town
Lone Dog's Winter Count
Iron Woman
Offering
One Age in a Dream

DRAMA
War Cries

ANTHOLOGIES
Braided Lives, An Anthology of Multicultural American Writing
Two Worlds Walking: Writers With Mixed Heritages

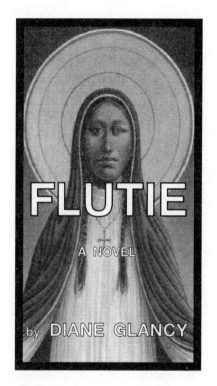

FLUTIE

A NOVEL

by DIANE GLANCY

MOYER BELL
Wakefield, Rhode Island & London

Gratefulness to Spencer Reece, Jim Turnure, Julie Klassen, Patricia Weaver Francisco, Jean Ferrar, and Barbara Banker for reading the manuscript, and as usual, Ruth Greenstein for her comments.

Acknowledgment to The Loft for a Career Initiative Grant which made possible the research trips to Oklahoma.

Thanks also to Macalester College for a Sabbatical during which I started the book.

Published by Moyer Bell

Copyright © 1998 by Diane Glancy
Jacket art: Blessed Kateri Tekakwitha by Fr. John Giuliani

First Edition

LIBRARY OF CONGRESS
CATALOGING IN PUBLICATION DATA

Glancy, Diane
    Flutie / by Diane Glancy. — 1st ed.

       p.   cm.
I. Title.
PS3557.L294F58   1998
813'.54-dc21   CIP
ISBN 1-55921-212-8   97-26593

Printed in the United States of America.
Distributed in North America by Publishers Group West,
P.O. Box 8843, Emeryville, CA 94662, 800-788-3123
(in California 510-658-3453)

There's the sky and the ground with
nothing between them but a landscape
of stories you can hear if you hold
your ear to the air to the land—

FLUTIE

Flutie

He makes the dumb to speak.
Mark 7:37

Remove the lump in my throat so I can speak.
Joe Swamp

I.

Flutie stood in Hampton's Garage in Vini, Oklahoma. Her brother, Franklin, was leaning into the engine of an old Plymouth working the butterfly valve with his finger. "Get in push the gas for me," Franklin said, and Flutie got into the car. She revved it when Franklin told her to, feeling the Plymouth lift and flutter. She felt her wings unfold. She flew over the wildflowers of the oil cans and fan belts. Past the studded walls of the garage.

She rode with Franklin on the highway. The tall grasses in the ditches flying by. Franklin listened to the motor of the Plymouth, but the wind was the only voice Flutie heard. The wind and the water from the dried sea that once had covered the Great Plains.

Sometimes Flutie heard the waves in the silence of her room. The sea was in her backyard. She felt the summer jumping on her face. The heat was like a foot stepping on her head. She wanted to say, *get off*, but when she tried to speak, the sea knew where she was. She felt the waves flood over her.

The roof slanted over her narrow bed in the attic of their house on the dirt road. She had chest of drawers. Her jeans and tee shirts on a nail. A picture of Jesus stuck on another nail, the edges curling in the heat. He was walking through a field.

Sometimes the county sheriff drove by the place.

"There'some reason he's watching you, Frank?" Flutie's mother asked.

"You sure he idn't waiting for you to tear out of here?" her father answered.

Sometimes Flutie slept on the glider on the back porch. Sometimes Franklin slept in their father's truck. She thought it looked like a submarine under the moon.

Sometimes in the night Flutie heard something. The truck pushed out of the yard, starting on the road, the headlights off. She saw the faint glimmer of its reflection under the moon like a submarine surfacing, then submerging again over the hill.

Flutie sat on the glider on the screened porch. She sat in the dark so quiet she could hear the angels fly in heaven. Far away, she heard her father's truck turn onto the highway. Somewhere a dog barked. Flutie thought the sound of the faraway truck was the sun turning on its engine before it heated up the land.

Flutie sweated even in the night. She must have been sleeping again when her father's truck came back into the yard. The next thing she heard was her mother's skillet on the stove.

Franklin looked at Flutie with his sleepy eyes. "What you sleeping on the porch for?" He pushed past her in the kitchen that was cluttered with car magazines and engine parts.

"The attic's hot," she said.

After her chores Flutie walked down the road. She passed Ruther and Luther's house, the old sister and brother. She saw Luther's mower in the dirt yard. She wanted to stop and talk, but she hummed now with something more than them. She was on the edge of some enormous quiet she wanted to transcend.

2.

Now Flutie felt the chalk-board against her back. She opened her mouth. She tried to talk in front of the class, but there was no air. The teacher looked at her. The students stared. Their eyes were fish eyes.

Her head felt full of water. If she tried to talk the words moved like waves on an ocean. She sat down. Her heart pounding. Her head bobbing from fright.

3.

The signs went by too fast to read on the way to Woodward with her mother. But Flutie knew what they said. Jackson's Auto Repair. Dennis Welding. Where was it Franklin went at night?

Flutie was small for her thirteen years, but her jeans were still short on her legs. Most girls wore jeans but Flutie wanted a dress. Once her mother tied an apron around her waist and from the front Flutie looked like she wore a dress. She ran in the yard turning one way and another to see the ruffle of the apron twirl.

Now in the second-hand store in Woodward, Flutie saw a dress. It was plaid. Made to wear in Heaven. For the Queen of Angels. "No," her mother said, but Flutie stood by the plaid dress with its short puffy sleeves and white yoke and sash. Her mother moved to the next rack. Flutie clutched the dress. She would not let go. When her mother called her, Flutie still clung to the dress. She stood frozen when her mother walked to her. She cowered as if her mother would slap her, but her mother took the dress with Flutie attached to it and went to the front counter to pay. That's what Flutie would remember. Her legs trembling as the woman put the dress in a brown sack. Flutie held it to her chest as they drove off in the truck, her mother shifting awkwardly jerking Flutie's neck.

They turned south on Highway 34. It was twenty miles to Vini. Her mother could drive it in less than eighteen minutes. Flutie hunched by the door and held her dress. She thought of the land rushing by. A horse in the front yard of a house. Tires on a fench-post. A sign, No Trespassing. Little roads with mail-boxes. The fields. Fences. Sky. Flutie knew they were there. When she was with her father she could see. Signs like Franklin had in his room. County road 71 16 13.20. Polled herefords. Posted warnings. Deer crossings.

The country was full. Scrub trees. Brush. Cedars. Hayrolls. Knolls. A front porch general store. Outbuildings. Storage bins. Aluminum sheds.

A farmtruck turned from a gravel road. Flutie's mother flew into the oncoming lane. Flutie closed her eyes. Dogs walking down dirt roads. A rag caught on a fence standing straight out in the wind. A small church. She went over the land in her mind so she wouldn't think of the road flying by. The red soil. Adams' farm. An old waterstorage tank.

They must be nearing Vini. T & R Services Rock Hauling. A sign, Dewey County 4 H. The roadside park with an outhouse. Carol's Trailer park. McNeill Construction. Water tower. The stop sign at Junction 60. Vini.

The sheriff didn't get her that time.

After the light was out that night, Flutie put on her dress and slept in it. It was wrinkled the next morning and her mother tried to take it off her to iron, but Flutie fought her mother again. After school her mother could iron it. "You can't iron something dirty," her mother said. "It settles the dirt." But Flutie waited for the schoolbus in her wrinkled dress, feeling the air on her legs. That's what dresses did to you. Let the air lick your knees. Now she had a dress with a sash that tied behind her. She could untie it and gallop before someone like a horse.

4.

The cars and trucks parked at an angle to the curb on the two blocks of Main Street in Vini, which was also Highway 60 through town. Flutie's mother kept hitting the curb. Sometimes Flutie braced herself as her mother turned to park.

"You get the wheels out of balance," Flutie's father told her.

"You work in the garage," she said. "You can straighten them."

Flutie liked the white plastered walls of the restroom in back of Hampton's Garage, the little round heater that buzzed in winter, the blue flowering vine that crept past the window in summer without looking.

Flutie's mother sat on the edge of the old desk when they stopped at the garage to see Flutie's father and brother. Flutie stood in the door looking into the glare of the afternoon sun.

Along the two rows of brick buildings on Main Street was a bank, a post office, *Feed and Seed* General Store and Hardware, Carpter's Drygoods, the Green Cafe and Grocer, City Hall, and a mortuary. Hampton's Garage waited at the east end of town. Across the street, the tall granary with its silos marked, *Farmer's Co-op*, stood like a mast over Vini.

After stopping at the grocer, Flutie and her mother started back to their place on a dirt road several miles west of Vini. They passed a small cluster of houses, the Baptist Church, and Speck Street which went to Vini's school three blocks south of Main. Flutie's mother pulled down the visor, barely catching a traffic ticket which fell, and squinted into the sun.

5.

It had not rained and the walls turned to dust. The upholstery on the two floral chairs withered. The rugs blew away. The spigot dried out and only coughed when Luther turned it on. *The electricity had to be turned off,* he reminded himself. *The dryness made a vacuum that would pull it out of the walls.*

Ruther, Luther's sister, thought she saw spirits in her chaise lounge. "The one," she said, "had flames for hair." She noticed how loosely its shoes were tied. *You're going to trip,* she wanted to say.

Ruther could hear the angels from the second rack of heaven. She saw the hereafter as the inside of an oven with racks and interior light. When the door was shut, it was dark, but when Ruther prayed, the door opened and she saw the tight ropes she had to walk.

Meanwhile, the houses shriveled. The petunias dried to a stalk, and the bushes bent to the ground. Their leaves curled like fists. Still Luther mowed the yard.

Ruther threw bread crumbs out the back door for the buffalo she thought were there. There were thousands of buffalo, she sometimes said, just as before. "Holy animals. You're scaring them away," she yelled to Luther. "You're out there mowing the yard, grunting louder than they do. Luther, shut that thing off! There's no grass in the yard to mow!"

Vini's oldest sister and brother, Ruther and Luther, were worried. They felt something happening. They didn't know what. Only the birds and animals seemed to know, but their tongues swelled in their mouths and they couldn't talk.

All day Ruther sang to the rain. She called it *hither*. Hither. The word had a sound to it that sounded. Rang, in other words.

She read about rain in other parts. *Rivers flooded and fields made a seabed*—Ruther spoke rain to the sky. *Rain you are falling.* She closed her eyes so hard she saw lightning. *Rain you are falling,* she repeated through the day.

Luther knew that Ruther would pray until the rain fell. It was because the earth was turning to dust. The curtains shrinking at the windows. The earth smelling like the bundt cake Ruther left in the oven while she walked the racks of heaven.

A cloud lifted around the house. Luther wore goggles when he mowed the dust. He breathed like a woman in labor.

"Luther, hold it down out there," Ruther said. But Luther still wheezed.

The goggles were two round circles with a thick rubber strap, the excess part sticking out at the buckle like an antennae behind his ear. The goggles looked like they came from outerspace or the *prediluvian* sea. Flutie had found the word in the library where she stayed sometimes after school to read.

Don't Resuscitate, was written on the door of the house. "You understand, Ruther? I been seeing the ancestors in them overstuffed chairs—the ones without their flowers nomore."

She shook her head.

"I hear a truck on the road at night," he said. "Somebody's going somewhere."

6.

Sometimes after school Flutie got off the bus to visit Franklin and her father at Hampton's Garage. Franklin was nearly five years older than Flutie. At eighteen, he still had a year of high school. He wouldn't let Flutie ride with him the few blocks from school. He wasn't always in school anyway.

Sometimes she watched the cars pass on Highway 60. It was just over fifty miles west to Texas. She wondered how it would be to cross the state line.

Franklin and their father worked on a '42 Ford coupe Franklin had found behind a house between Woodward and Fort Supply. It was a car Flutie's father remembered. He'd quit school and gone to Oklahoma City in a car like it. He'd worked in a salvage yard and scrap-metal place where the foreman pressed the men flatter than the cars. The men had families and had to work, and the foreman made it hard for them. Her father had talked back to him and was fired, and came back to Vini. Flutie's father was still looking for a ride in that car.

Mr. Hampton lived in Woodward and had a garage there too. Flutie's father and brother ran the Hampton Garage in Vini. Flutie's father wanted to buy the garage. It was just an old building with a hydraulic lift and gas pumps. Most of the tools were Flutie's father's.

Everyone's car or tractor or truck was old. Maybe once in a while someone got a new truck, but there was almost always a car in the garage that needed repair. When there wasn't, Flutie's father restored the hull and engine of the '42 Ford. Sometimes

Franklin's friends were there. Flutie was afraid of them, their long hair and jeans, their leather jackets, their language.

Once they had let her ride with them in their highway parade of custom cars. Riding beside Franklin, Flutie had felt the high rack of Ruther's heaven.

Sometimes Flutie's father let her hold a wrench or another tool he would need. Usually she threw rocks at the trellis of primrose, or the barrels of oil cans and trash and worn-out parts behind the garage. Someone had planted the roses years ago which kept coming up by themselves. Also the blue flowering vine that climbed the back of the garage.

Sometimes Flutie saw Franklin take a hood ornament for his collection. Anyone with a new car would soon be missing the ornament. He also had a collection of license plates and highway markers. They were all in Franklin's room. One morning she woke with him banging on the wall. He was making shelves for the hood ornaments. Anyone stopping in town would drive away without their ornament. The boys would stand in front of the car while the people were in the Green Cafe. Sometimes Flutie knew the boys went to Woodward, maybe farther. Sometimes she knew Franklin drove off at night.

The sheriff floated in and out of Flutie's sight as she popped rocks at the barrels. She heard her father argue with Franklin but she didn't know why they argued. Flutie saw Franklin stomp off toward their dirt road. She went into the garage.

"You could tell me a story," Flutie said as she watched her father under a car. He shrugged and shook his head as if thinking, *there were no stories left.* He had to drop them. The way ships threw cargo overboard in a storm. The way the wagons moving west had to leave trunks and furniture.

What could he give her? Just one story? she asked.

Not even that. He adjusted the brakes on the car.

"Can I make up a story?" She asked.

"Do what you want," he said. "Your grandmother had nothing but stories."

Flutie wanted him to say something else. She wanted him to say that stories didn't mean anything. Their history was better left unsaid. All the changing. All the loss. But she knew he wasn't thinking about stories any longer.

She knew nothing about her father before he went to Oklahoma City and came back to Vini. Most of the Moses family had disappeared that way. Left their Cherokee heritage. Just walked off down the road and no one ever saw them again.

Flutie didn't know what brought her father back. He could have gone someplace else, anywhere but Vini. When he returned, he married a woman he met at the Baptist Church social. He named his son Franklin. His daughter Florence, though he called her Flutie after that. Flutie thought the Christian God would give her words. But she couldn't keep her thoughts on the sermons on Sundays.

Sometimes her father hunted a deer and dressed it in a shed behind a neighbor's house. Then the old ways came back. She tried to make a story.

There was a deer in the woods.

The words were wild in her mouth like the taste of venison. She watched her father skin the deer. There was grace in its wide-eyed silence.

7.

Flutie's mother sped on the highway, over the hilly, rust-red soil, and the sandy basin of the old sea. Flutie liked the Canadian River valley near Taloga, some thirty miles southeast of Vini. Taloga had just over 400 people. Half of Vini. A third of Woodward. Flutie thought nearly all 400 must watch her mother buzz through town. "You're going to get stopped again," Flutie said. Her mother shot words that hit her. Flutie picked them up from the floorboard and put them in her mouth. She chewed the brass casing of a cartridge. The old bullet sky at dusk. She fingered her tongue. The two blood drops of her eyes.

8.

"How do you get to Seiling?" A man stopped his car on the street as Flutie walked up Main. She turned to look down the road. She tried to say, *straight ahead,* but she just pointed. Her head dropped. She looked at her feet in shame. Ruther Rutherford had been shopping at the grocer's. She came out and pointed east down Highway 60. "Maybe twenty miles," she said. The woman in the car still looked at Flutie as the man drove off.

"You can talk to people, Flutie," Ruther said. "That was just some man asking directions. Open your mouth and feel those little words run out."

9.

There was a rock buried in the road. Sometimes Flutie could see it after a wash-out. But rain didn't come that often or hard in western Oklahoma. She liked knowing the rock was there. It was a barrier. A protector. Only those who were supposed to be on the road knew it was there. The schoolbus, the mailtruck and grain trucks, the people who lived in farmhouses and trailers along the road — Ruther and Luther and the other neighbors in a long and spread-out line. Something like sheets in the backyards hanging up to dry.

Nothing else could be counted on. Except poverty and her father's distance when she wanted to know about him. When she wanted him to tell his stories.

But when he thought she wasn't listening, then she'd hear. Sometimes Flutie felt something in her ear. The words that had been lost? If she waited long enough while he worked in the garage, he'd start humming to himself. He'd found rectangle parking lights for his '42 Ford and was mounting them above the grille. Flutie could hear the voices around him. Voices of an old language. Sometimes he didn't seem to hear them and they'd be out of tune. Other times they spoke together. Even after she told him what she'd heard, he told her there were no stories left.

Sometimes even her mother had another language. Old German words she'd heard her grandmother say. *Ist ja wieder gut.* Flutie'd hear something like that. *Everything will be all right.*

Flutie imagined the rock kept the road from sinking into the underground sea. She imagined the rock held up the fields along the road. The farmhouses and trailers. In fact, she imagined the rock held up all of Oklahoma from the aquifer that tried to climb above the land. Flutie could feel it sometimes at night. The house seemed to rock like a boat.

10.

Flutie's father put his arm on the back of the seat, and Flutie moved toward him. The truck had a knob on the steering wheel so Flutie's father could turn with one hand. As they drove toward Vini, Flutie saw the granary on the edge of town, the heat waves, the railroad track.

The parts of Vini were like words of a story she

wanted to tell. But the words in her head buckled on her tongue before she could say them. The old buildings had voices. The feed and seed store. The gas pump and Hampton's Garage with oil stains on the ground that looked like spirits to Flutie, when their spotted wings unfolded. The whole town had voices. Flutie could hear them when she passed.

The sheriffs from Dewey and Woodward Counties were parked at Hampton's. They were talking to Beatrix, the schoolbus driver.

"What do they want?" Flutie's father frowned.

"Franklin's tightening the clutch on the bus," Flutie said. "They're just talking."

The brightness of the sun hit the *Farmers' Co-op* sign on the granary silos by Hampton's. It was broken as much by the light as by the dust rising from the traffic that came to town.

Flutie's father had to decide which way to turn. He decided to head to the Green Cafe.

Flutie sat in the window of the cafe with her father. He was talking to some men about the oil rigs in trouble because of the oversea's market. Or he talked about cars, looking over his shoulder at the garage. How to reconstruct fenders. How to find the parts they needed. The '42 Ford had parking lights in the body instead of on top of the fenders. He'd nearly had to use the mounted ones, but Franklin had found the inset ones somewhere.

Sometimes her father's friends tried to talk to her. It made her heart pound and she looked down at her lap until they went on with their conversation. Flutie saw she'd spilled something on the white yoke of her dress. She wanted to cover it with her hand. Sometimes she couldn't speak because of her shyness. Other times she just didn't have anything to say.

11.

There was a time long ago. It was hard to remember. What had caused it to happen?

She was running in the yard. Something fluttered over her head. A spirit being. Or an angel. Flutie didn't know who she was. She had no memory of seeing her, but she could describe her. She had pigtails and beaded shoes. She wore trousers like Flutie always had to, but she also wore a dress. Flowers grew from her feet. A disk flew at her head like a flag. The spirit was watching her—but she must have looked away.

Somehow Flutie cut her face and tongue. The blood was warm as her mother's hand. She was running after Franklin and something hit. She didn't know what. Maybe she ran into the tractor and its sharp seat. It gashed her and they took her to the doctor and he wrapped her in a sheet and they held her down and sewed up her head and tongue. It was the hospital in Woodward. The doctor looked like Donald Duck in his white coat and mask. The terror unzipped her face. The pain was like the sun.

She still dreamed of it. *Sometimes a doctor in white came in the door and she sat up in her attic bed, hitting her head on the slanting roof. Chop shop. Chop shop. Say that fast five times. The duck was talking. The others were wrapping her up. The white waves of the ocean driving themselves into her face.*

12.

Swallow rode the schoolbus with Flutie. Her family lived on the same dirt road as the Moses's. She'd ridden to Hampton's Garage with her father, Mr. Smots, in their old car.

"The aerial on your truck—" Swallow started

to say and then Flutie couldn't remember what happened. They were both dazed.

Sometimes lightning seemed to dance on the prairie before a storm, and dust would lift toward the sky. It must have been a stray piece of lightning by the garage—

"What were you standing out in the open for?" Flutie's father asked. For a moment, the wind seemed to sweep the garage away. They hid their faces from the flying dirt.

Swallow said she saw the truck aerial quiver and heard it snap. "Maybe the air was wired," Franklin said, looking at her. Swallow and her father waited until the wind died down and the storm was nothing more than a few large splats. Then they left.

But something had slipped. Weren't they always afraid of falling off into space? The land was thin as ice over a pond. Isn't that what happened to Flutie's father's brother and sisters when they walked off down the road? They had the sky and the land with nothing to hold onto. At any time they could slip off the earth.

But Flutie wasn't afraid of the sky. She was afraid of the underground water. Sometimes she dreamed she was in a dark sea. Lightning couldn't get her there. She rubbed her hand over her face that still felt numb, but she only felt the old scar.

She'd been baptized in the creek several years ago. The cars driving there after church parked in a line on the road. But she'd choked somehow in the shallow creek and came out of the water coughing.

The fish were planets looking at her from underwater. It was quiet in space. It was quiet underwater. Only on land did someone have to talk. Her teacher knew she couldn't speak in front of others. It seemed at times she arranged for Flutie to slip into terror. Then she watched Flutie panic. Her speaking came from choking, her breath bursting into her after being underwater too long. The teacher waiting to see her fear ripen.

13.

After her father dressed a deer, Flutie kept a scrap of the hide. She made antlers from twigs and walked around the yard beyond the trees where they couldn't see. She spoke in the silence.

Her feet told a story in the leaves. When she stood still, she could hear her breath like the hiss of the ocean that had once covered the plains. She could still feel the water. She made the dance of a deer swimming.

When she was in school, the leaves threw a tantrum in the school yard. *Hey wind,* she could yell for the wind to carry her away too, but her throat would close as if a large hand clamped it. She felt the heat of her shame. It was red as the heart of the deer. Outside the school somebody rode away on his motorcycle. Somebody was free.

She could talk to someone she knew, if she didn't think about it. But she had never been able to speak to someone she didn't know, or in a group when she had to.

Maybe back in the woods where the deer lived, the trees moved like great long tongues.

She didn't have anyone to talk to. She couldn't, anyway. It was as if she had her mouth sewn shut.

Maybe the air would be her friend.

In a dream she saw a sweat lodge, red from the heat within. She felt the choking already closing her throat like a hand.

She thought of a story of a ship that moved on the ocean. She had read stories of the ocean in books. Sometimes she heard the ocean that had covered the

Great Plains of America. It had dried up in the Salt Plains near Jet, Oklahoma. Her voice moved inside her like a boat. She could feel the waves dashing the shore of the room. if she could speak a story, she would have a way across the water. But she stayed on the dock and turned back to the empty road. What was that? A tree? What stubbed against her foot?

There was a red heat in her. She knew it in school when the teacher talked about an underwater volcano spitting lava into the ocean. Yes. How the water boiled. That's what she felt.

It was what she spoke. Not words. But tears. Melted words. She was a sweat-lodge rock in the morn. And under the tears was her anger in knowing that she couldn't talk when it counted.

Sometimes in the darkness inside her head, she could see an opening above her. She could see figures looking down at her from the opening. They were Elders. Helpers. She knew it. Maybe they were the Indian people of her father's tribe who were gone, but they were still there.

Flutie heard her mother and father argue about the sweat lodge in their backyard. Her mother didn't want it, but her father said it was the only part of his heritage he had left, and he was going to keep it.

Flutie felt hope rise against the feeling that she would never have anywhere to belong. Sometimes her thoughts burned in her head.

14.

If Jesus was her savior she could dart around heaven with fins and shark teeth. Instead, she sat in her backyard, dressing some rocks she'd found with string. Wrapping it around them and around them, pulling tightly as she could.

Sometimes at night she shined a flashlight on them. Then they made rock stories larger than the dark. Somewhere in the Salt Plains near Jet, her teacher said, there were rocks made of salt crystals where the old sea had dried up. Flutie thought if she were there, she could hear them speak from the ancient sea.

15.

Flutie's father saw that the truck was covered with dust. Flutie heard the chair scrape in the kitchen. Franklin was backing away from his father.

"You got the truck out at night?"

Then they went at it. Flutie ran from the back porch letting the screen door bang several times. She walked down the road to Ruther and Luther's. She sat in the chaise lounge in the backyard until Ruther would see her and invite her in for grits.

16.

There was a woman who stopped at the Green Cafe. She was wild like a deer. She came in, paused a moment while everyone looked at her, and sat at a table by the window. She ordered iced coffee and a sandwich. She was a graceful woman. It's why she could travel on her own. No man at first knew what to do about her. By the time they decided she'd moved on. But the woman ate self-consciously at times, Flutie thought while she watched her.

The woman had stories falling from her. Flutie

picked some of them up. Where had she come from? Where was she going? Was she one of the magic people? One from the other world? How did a woman get to travel by herself? If Flutie held out her thumb, would she take Flutie with her? Why would she pass through Vini? Was she one of those trickster spells that let you see yourself at a later age, way down the road?

"We could custom that without any trouble." Franklin and his friends were looking at the woman's car. Talking about it as if it were theirs to talk about. "Look at that orn," one of Franklin's friends said.

Flutie moved to a table at the window when one of Franklin's friends left the cafe. She watched him walk by the woman's car. Flutie went outside. "If you take that ornament I'm going to tell her."

"You little shit what can you do?" And with a chop of something in his hand, the ornament was gone from the hood of the car. "Keep your nose on your own face," he said and walked off.

Franklin, leaving the cafe, pushed by her.

When the woman finished her lunch she stood at the counter and paid, then drove off in her road car without its ornament. She must have known, Flutie thought, and watched the empty hole where her car had disappeared down Highway 60 west from Vini.

17.

Flutie saw some girls walking toward her on Main Street. She turned into Carpter's Drygoods so she wouldn't have to talk to them.

"Well, Flutie, how are you?" Mr. Carpter said.

"Fine," Flutie answered and went back to the street, passing the girls as if she were in a hurry and couldn't speak.

18.

The Baptist minister was a literalist.

"God made a dome and separated the waters that were below the dome from the waters that were above the dome." Genesis 1:7.

Dome, in Hebrew, means, *raki'a*, a beaten sheet of metal. Yes, heaven is sheet metal. It's in the Word, therefore it is. The space ships are searching to find the waters above the beaten sheet of metal, which is the sky the space ships fly through looking for the water. Maybe the metal sky opens like a lock in a canal when ships pass. Somehow the space ships get through.

"Then God made lights in the dome of heaven," the minister went on.

Flutie imagined the ceiling light in her father's truck where she tried to read sometimes when Franklin and his friends were in his room. Then she imagined the ceiling light which hung on its cord in her attic room. Jesus walked in the wheat field there.

"The stars must be like yardlights on their posts," the minister was thinking to himself as he talked.

"Or maybe the metal is further away. Far far away. That's it. The sheet metal is out in outer space beyond our solar system. You know that tinny sound you hear sometimes in the openness? That's the space ships trying to get through." The minister took a breath.

Out in the churchyard after the sermon, Ruther shook her head. "The water above the heavens is just the clouds," she said, "nothing more than vapor. Where does he get that nonsense?"

"He's giving us a report from earth," Luther

said. "The moon of earth wouldn't be a light at all, if you looked at it from Mars."

No, the Bible was given to us on earth from earth. For a certain place and time. We needed the words of its story. Because we were stories.

19.

Open my mouth that I might speak. That was what she wanted each year in school. Release. Something like the pines that wandered from the cemetery, their seeds taking to the sandy Oklahoma soil. Flutie wanted space. She wanted flight. She wanted something more than she had.

She felt it when she rode in her brother's car. Or when she saw a deer jump a fence, graceful as if there were no effort at all, graceful as if it had wings. It jumped the road. Then disappeared.

Flutie could race too. Into the air. Fluttering like an angel or a leaf from the tree by the neighbor's shed. Maybe she would become the deer. Maybe she would be skinned. She thought of the knife slitting her neck and her back along her spine.

She had a friend, Jess Tessman. He was taller

than she was. He was her age, but whenever Franklin saw him with Flutie, he made a lunge toward him as if they were boxing. Why did he always do that?

She felt Franklin would skin her. There was something about him that scared her. Maybe it was because he was stronger and liked to push himself. Maybe it was because her father always pushed him. Flutie decided she wouldn't hold still like the deer. But the deer was dead and she was alive. Yes, that was it.

She ran after Jess in the pasture behind his house. His father had some land and a few head of cattle down another dirt road west of Vini. Something had happened to Jess' mother. Flutie couldn't remember. She was gone and Jess' father stayed to himself.

They were all poor in western Oklahoma. There was only the hope of marrying, having children, and continuing the struggle with her nose pushed into the dirt. She wanted to go to Southwestern Oklahoma State University in Weatherford. There'd been a career day at school. Flutie had listened to the college students talk. She'd heard the word *geology*.

Flutie wanted to know the names of rocks. She

wanted to move across the land with her words. Her stories were her car. Let Franklin box with Jess. Let Franklin drive off. Let him speed over the hill like their mother, swerving around the rock in the road. Let him make cars from nothing. Let him go with his friends to the car shows and swappers and old-cars-for-sale corrals and leave her behind. Flutie could make stories with her words. If only she could speak.

20.

Franklin wanted to quit school and his father wouldn't let him. He was nineteen years old, nearly twenty, and he wasn't going back. They argued about it in the mornings when Flutie's mother slammed the skillet on the stove. Flutie was already fifteen. She was going to pass him in school.

Franklin's friends had quit, he argued. He wasn't going to be the oldest in school. He held his head with a hangover.

"A lot of them kids are older," his mother said. "They got to help with the haying. They can't always hide in the library reading them books." Flutie's mother looked at her.

Franklin's father wouldn't let up. If Franklin finished high school, he could go to college and learn accounting. They could buy the garage and run it. They wouldn't always be at a loss.

Franklin tried to eat his eggs with his father yelling in his face. He would leave Vini, he said. He would go to Fort Sill in Lawton and join the army.

"How'd you make it in the army? You can't even get out of bed in the morning." Franklin's father threw his toast at Franklin. Franklin flung his plate at his father.

"Get out of here, Franklin," Flutie's mother said, "you're going too far."

Franklin bolted from the kitchen and roared down the road in his truck as Flutie's mother wrestled with her husband to hold him in the kitchen.

Later that evening, when Flutie returned from Ruther and Luther's, Flutie's father put the tarp over the sweat-lodge frame in the backyard. He built a fire in the pit and heated the rocks.

When Franklin came back drunk, Flutie's father dragged Franklin into the sweat lodge. Flutie listened to Franklin yell as his father pounded him. She heard him plead to get out of the sweat lodge that was hotter than his father's anger, hotter than their feeling of hopelessness, hotter than the failure that hedged them on the western Oklahoma plains.

She heard Franklin get sick. She heard her father cry.

Her mother sat in the kitchen holding a wet rag over her dark eye.

21.

Beatrix drove the bus hard as she always did. Flutie rode behind Swallow. Sometimes Flutie watched Swallow's hair flying in the air. Once Swallow turned as Flutie was looking at her. "We're sisters of the lightning," Swallow said.

Swallow was a year behind Flutie in school, though she looked like she was a year ahead. Swallow could sing in church and in school. She could be baptized and not choke.

Flutie sat behind her on the bus. Swallow got off at the mailbox marked, *Philip Fred Smots.* Then Flutie rode past the Rutherford box to the Moses'. Swallow's family had a garden that dried up by July and a few head of cattle. Her father had a well dug with some money they'd had. Swallow's mother wouldn't talk to him because it was the only money they'd had. But later, when people bought the water from them, it was the only income they had.

Swallow was the second of several daughters. Her name was Susan Sandra, but her family called her Swallow. Her oldest sister lived in Woodward with a husband and several children. Swallow had her father's bright eyes and mother's light hair. *She's a streamer,* Flutie heard her father say once as she drove the tractor. There was nothing he could do. Western Oklahoma was hot and dry. Hopeless of ever being anything. But it's where they were from. It was the land where their grandparents had come during the land run. It was theirs. Nothing else was certain.

If only Flutie could cut out cardboard sections of her life, stand them upright in the dust like rock, number them like road signs in Frank's room.

Sometimes Flutie read as the bus tossed down the dirt road and swerved to miss the rock. She read about a man who cut out a woman's tongue. He'd raped her and didn't want her to tell because he was married to her sister.

Philomela couldn't talk, but she wove her story in a tapestry so her sister, Procne, would know. In a rage, Procne killed her son and fed him to the husband who'd raped her sister. She fled to Philomela, but when her husband followed, they turned into birds.

Flutie thought of the woman she'd seen in the Green Cafe. Maybe she was Philomela. Flying in her car like a bird. Without a tongue. But the woman had ordered coffee and a sandwich. But Flutie hadn't heard her voice.

Now Flutie had a story, she thought. *A deer came from the woods. It had a mouth but couldn't talk.*

She thought about her story later, when she was sitting in the back of the classroom. When she heard her brother and his friends. When she heard her father and mother and Franklin fighting.

The deer was silent as a fish. It had no tongue. But its silence was a story.

Flutie wanted to speak. She wanted to stand in front of the class and tell the story. But fear flooded her throat. She could talk in her house. She could talk to Ruther and Luther. If there was just one or two. But in front of everyone when she had to—nothing could be said. It was as if she stood over herself with a ruler beating.

In the classroom the rows of chairs were waves. She looked at her lap. Her face burned as if she had stood near a volcano. Others were watching. She had tried to speak but sank into herself. How do you speak from underwater? She would never come out.

Other times she rolled around in herself like a marble. She had a voice somewhere inside her. She could feel it moving.

Flutie continued her story. *There was a deer who lived under the water.*

There was a place in her that could speak. Sometimes she imagined it. Others would be listening. She would give them her hands. She would give them her feet like two ragged deer-hide bags.

There was a deer whose name was Philomela.

22.

Flutie put the plates on the table in the evening. Her mother said. "You aren't going nowhere doing a sloppy job like that."

Flutie banged a plate and it broke. Her father took off his belt and swatted her legs. She ran upstairs to her room. He followed her and swatted until the sting made her yelp for him to stop.

In the night she heard her own voice. *That's*

what hardship did to her father. It made him angry sometimes. It made him do things Flutie knew he didn't choose to do. It seemed all he ever did anymore was argue with Franklin. It had turned him sour.

23.

Swallow was a girl every boy wanted but Franklin got her with his car. He could take apart engines and after a few trials, he could have them running. He had a sense of motors. He knew the parts. He knew how things connected. Working with his father in the garage somehow fueled his skill. That's what held him to Hampton's.

In the garage Franklin looked greased in his tee shirt and work jeans. But in the hot breeze and light sun that came in the wide door, he was separate auto parts that had been connected and made whole.

Swallow saw this and sat on the hood of the car while he worked underneath. She had on shorts and a halter top and Franklin couldn't keep his eyes off her legs. He kept watching the mound of her ankle bone and her toes in their sandals. It was dirty in the garage and her feet were dusty. As if she grew out of the land, as if the land claimed her first and he got what was left. He could use his tongue to make a path in the dust on her foot.

She tried to get away but not much. She'd had a boyfriend in Taloga and she watched him in the field. But nothing ever came of it.

"I could help you," Swallow said.

"What do you know about engines?"

"I know sometimes they won't work and you need to fix them."

"You've got to know what you're doing."

"I could hold the wrench. Find the grease rag."

"You'd get dirty."

"I could just sit here."

"I could come to the car show with you," Swallow said another afternoon.

"How do you know I'm going?" Franklin asked.

"I heard you say so."

"I can't get the engine finished in time."

"You'll go anyway with your friends."

Flutie rode between her parents in her father's truck to the car show in Elk City. Swallow rode with Franklin and his friends in a long line of old cars.

Flutie walked with them through the rows of cars in the hot field. Sometimes Flutie listened to their words. *Cylinder heads. Hold-down clamps. Intake bolts. Connecting rods.* Sometimes they'd laugh and look at Swallow and Flutie. They'd walk and say, *spark timing, screw-in rocker plates,* comments like that.

Flutie saw other girls look at Franklin and his friends. The boys were sleek and black in their leather vests. It scared Flutie to look at their bare chests. She saw other girls over-powered by their beauty. Was that the word? Beauty?

A man covered with tattoos walked by in his undershirt. "There's someone for you, Flutie," Franklin said, and his friends laughed.

The heat made Flutie dizzy and she sat on the running board of a sedan. She looked at the cars. A '40 Ford panel truck. A '48 Chevy delivery. The earth cracked under her feet with sparse patches of smothered grass.

She saw Franklin talking to some girl whose jean-shorts were ripped up the sides.

24.

"I could still come to the dance," Franklin told Swallow back in Hampton's Garage. She didn't say anything and he looked at her.

"Flutie and Jess could ride with us?" she asked. "This is their last year."

"No," he looked at her.

"You could have finished high school if you'd read something other than your car magazines," Swallow answered, and walked away with Flutie. "It's like Frank has a bag of anger over his head," she said.

"He got it from our dad," Flutie answered. "Something's ahead of him on the road and he can't get around it. The road's too narrow for him to pass and he's eating dust."

Swallow moved on to someone else. And Franklin married Geneva, whose car he repaired after their mother sideswiped it.

25.

Geneva was two years older than Franklin. She'd come from a rural family somewhere around Vini. Franklin remembered her in school. She had spaces between her teeth and Flutie listened to her talk as she clomped down the stairs helping Franklin move out. They would live in the trailer park on the edge of Vini. Franklin drove his truck slowly away from the house. Then Flutie sat on the bed in her attic room holding her box of rocks, the silence ringing her ears.

26.

Flutie's father and brother were going to a large salvage yard near Cleo Springs. She heard them at supper. Flutie found it on the map. Nearly a day's trip there and back. She'd never been that far from Vini. Flutie followed the map with her finger. Highway 412 east from Woodward. Highway 8 north past Cleo Springs. She kept going. Highway 64 west. The Great Salt Plains!

"I want to go," Flutie said.

"The truck'd be crowded," Franklin said.

"A teacher talked about the Salt Plains once," Flutie insisted. "I'd ride in back."

"The wind would blow you away," her father said.

"Take her," Flutie's mother said.

"Indians came to the Salt Plains. Then settlers took wagonloads of salt. In World War II, it was a strafing and bombing range." Flutie talked as she sat between her father and brother on the way to Cleo Springs.

"Listen to the teacher," Franklin mocked.

"Now it belongs to the birds, Franklin—the plovers—"

"Shut up, Flutie," Franklin said.

Flutie's father and brother found the parts they needed while Flutie waited by the truck.

Franklin took the wheel then. He started to turn south on Highway 8.

"I want to see the Salt Plains. You said I could."

"I didn't say anything," Franklin said.

"We're almost there—" Flutie felt a panic that she wouldn't get to go.

"You're trouble," Franklin said, and headed south from the salvage yard.

"Let's see the Salt Plains, Frank," Flutie's father said.

"I ain't got time."

"Franklin," Flutie pleaded.

"Geneva will be waiting in the trailer in her apron turning flapjacks."

"Turn around, Frank," their father said.

Franklin kept going.

Flutie felt a rage at him.

Their father grabbed the wheel. Franklin hit his hand away. Their father grabbed the wheel again. Franklin tried to jerk away from him, making his elbow fly in Flutie's face. For a moment she saw a sparkling blackness. Then a circle of light like the moon.

Franklin nearly ran off the road. His father grabbed him by the neck. "Turn this truck around." Franklin jerked the wheel and spun the truck in the middle of the road, hardly looking for traffic.

Flutie was crying, trying not to make a sound.

Her father looked at her face. "She'll have a shiner."

*   *   *

Franklin turned down a dirt road where a sign pointed to the Salt Plains. Flutie could see it in the distance—a flat gray field, thousands of acres, barren as the moon, marching toward the horizon to the northeast. Franklin drove the truck between the roped-off areas to the digging point.

Flutie got out. She dug the salt crystals with her fingers, wrapping them in a rag she found in the truck. Franklin stood there smoking, looking at the sky. Flutie's father brought some tools from the truck for her to dig with.

"It smells like manure," Franklin said as they left.

No wonder Flutie didn't have much to say. The land didn't speak much either. The earth, the sky, the dry creeks, the rows of trees between the fields. There were shades of green from the dark cedars to sun-bleached prairie grass. There were shades of brown from the russet red soil to the pale wheat fields.

They crossed the shallow Cimarron River. They crossed Griever Creek.

They passed Bud's Salvage and turned west on

Highway 412 back toward Woodward, some fifty miles away.

They passed the glass mountains and red mesas. Here were the *voicings*, Flutie thought, the tongues of the land, speaking in short bursts of courage before the wind blew the words back into their mouths. Her eye throbbed. The birds rising on air currents above the bluffs were the words that the land said. Sometimes Flutie watched the low brush country from the window of the truck, the bramble and shinnery.

Franklin whistled sometimes as he drove. It was a harsh, cruel sound. Flutie held the salt crystals in her hand, a darkening place under her eye.

The Salt Plains were the giant mouth where everything was swallowed. The sink where the ocean had drained with a sob stiffled in its chest.

27.

The rectangular parking lights on her father's Florentine blue 1942 Ford Super DeLuxe sedan coupe were gone. First one disappeared, then the other. Franklin found a parking light at a salvage yard somewhere and said he'd find another. He sold them to his father, who argued with him about it at first.

"I had to buy them," Franklin told his father. And Franklin's father would pay. One of the parking lights was from another make of car. It didn't match, but you didn't know it unless you had an eye for it. *It looks the same to me,* Flutie said.

28.

Flutie was at the Green Cafe when she heard Franklin and her father's voices carrying all the way from Hampton's Garage. Her father was shouting something and Flutie knew it was more than the other arguments they'd had. It was more serious than Franklin quitting school, which was the mistake her father had made. This time they were really fighting. Not just scuffling. This time Franklin was probably sober, not weakened by drunkenness.

Flutie ran to the garage to find her father and Franklin locked arm in arm. "Stop!" "Stop," she shouted. She was afraid Franklin would hurt him, but it was her father who had fury on his side. It was all Franklin could do to keep himself from being thrown on the ground. What was her father mad about? She'd never seen his fury this strong.

Flutie heard the sheriff's siren. Some men helped separate Flutie's father and brother. Franklin was arrested and put in the back of the sheriff's car. Flutie stood frozen with her hands in her mouth. She saw Jess Tessman, but she looked away from him. Geneva was there too.

"What happened?" Flutie asked.

Geneva said Franklin stole the auto parts, the air making sounds between her teeth. The sheriff had been at their place. Flutie ran behind the garage and pounded the barrels with rocks. The sheriff drove off with Franklin in the backseat. Everyone from the Green Cafe stood in the middle of the highway. The whole town seemed to come to a halt.

29.

Franklin was sentenced to two years in the prison at Stringtown.

"He won't be feeding me anymore with my own parts," Flutie's father said to Flutie and her mother as they ate supper in the kitchen.

Later Flutie sat in the window in her attic room under the sky, blue as her father's '42 Ford.

Down the road Luther snored in his house. Ruther sat in the yard speaking to the rain. *Rain*, she said. Clouds puffed into the sky. Small broken gray ones, as if their weatherboarded house were breaking up and the pieces were clouds hanging over her.

Flutie heard the thunder. She looked above the pitchfork trees. She saw a few clouds like shingles floating in the sky.

30.

Flutie's mother roared over the highways to Woodward, population 12,000, back through Vini, population 800, down toward Taloga, population 400.

The fields, population 19,000 cattle.

The sky, 49,000 birds.

The setting sun, an apple yellow.

Flutie's mother shifted suddenly. The small carton of milk Flutie was drinking from spilled in her father's truck.

Ist ja wieder gut.

Flutie heard her mother's German words, but she never heard her mother talk about her parents, or grandparents, or her past, either. It was as if they didn't exist. She lived only in the moment with nothing behind her. As she drove she rushed away from the past so it wouldn't catch up with her.

31.

Flutie's father stood in the garage eating an ice-cream sandwich. It looked like a car pressed flat in the scrap-metal yard. Flutie's father worked on the '42 Ford. She knew it was to forget Franklin. No, he couldn't forget him. It wasn't that. But to ease the anger and helplessness.

The grille on the original Ford was stainless steel stampings. Not die casting, because of the war. Flutie's father took off the die casting Franklin had installed, and her father restored the grille.

There were sheet metal splash pans connecting to the body. No running boards, but rubber stone guards on the rear fenders. Taillights were switched to horizontal.

Flutie listened to her father work in the garage.

She got in the front seat. She polished the fuel, oil, amp, and temp gauges. The clock and the glove box.

There was a wood-paneled '46 Ford station wagon in Seiling that outshone it, Flutie thought, but she didn't tell her father.

32.

Flutie and Jess stopped in his truck at the historical marker on Highway 60. "Let's get off the road," Jess said. "Your mother might be coming from town this time of afternoon."

1874
Cattle ranchers drove their herds through Western Indian Territory to a railhead at Dodge City, Kansas. Over 11,000,000 head of long-horn passed over the trail. The wake is marked by depressions worn into the land. To the south, you can see the U-shaped notch running through the sandy ridge to the Cherokee strip to the north.

Jess held his ear to the ground. He said he could still hear them. *Moooooo,* he answered the prairie wind that always sounded like the sea.

33.

Now Flutie and Jess ran down to the pond to a boat. He said, "Wait. The snakes. Don't get in. Not now. I feel them."

Flutie looked at him. She had no feelings like that, but she agreed, "Let's go back."

The hair was standing up on her arm. It was only then she felt chilled.

Flutie never knew what happened that day. Why that strange feeling came over her. Or why Jess felt it first. But something was there. A dock or landing pad from the past? Some old tribe in the brush? A ghost of someone who had died there? The whole land was haunted. The whole land talked. It called her again. She looked at the sky. She felt like she was seeing the bottom of an ocean through a clear plastic canopy.

Maybe she felt the voices of her father's family who'd gone off and were never seen again. Maybe it was Jess' mother. "Do you think people come back when they die?" she asked Jess.

He shook his head. "Nobody comes back after they leave. Even if they don't die. They're in Oklahoma City or Tulsa. In missions. In the streets," Jess said. "You just stay in Vini," he finished.

Maybe it was the mood of Jess' father she felt. He was so clamped to the place that he seemed to fill every open space.

One night Flutie stood at her window. Something was happening. She put on her jeans and shirt and went to the road.

Somewhere under the heavens, somewhere, something was happening. But she couldn't see it. The prairie was in her way. The whole world groaned in Western Oklahoma. The emptiness sucked the sounds into itself. A child dying in Africa. A woman crying in Bangladesh. Franklin turning in his bed in Stringtown. A man without hope in Wales. *Russians flatten a Chechan village*—Flutie had read the newspapers in the Green Cafe. She had seen the guns aimed and ready to fire. She could feel the whole world fighting. She could watch, but she was not part of it. Maybe she never would be. But she stood on the dirt road in the dark waiting for someone to come. Maybe the woman she'd seen in the Green Cafe. Or maybe Flutie would change into a nightingale and leave Western Oklahoma. She held her arms out as if they were wings, but she didn't fly anywhere.

She wouldn't ride with just anyone. They'd have to be going someplace where something was happening. Maybe she was waiting for the ghost of one of those drovers who'd pass through the land.

No, she wasn't waiting for a cowboy. And she wasn't waiting for Jess. Jess wasn't her man. She felt the disappointment.

Flutie wanted a mechanic. A restorer of cars. She wanted to feel like she did when she rode with her father in the Florentine blue Ford. *Where are you?* she thought. *In some garage under a '37 Buick? Get yourself up. Get your jeans out here. I'm waiting for you. We're going to ride down the highway and jump off the edge of the earth. Poke a hole up there and let the water fall through.*

What was the name of heaven when the Baptist minister talked about it? Something like Ruther's rack of heaven. The cattleguard.

34.

Sometimes Flutie had dreams that kept her inside them. The barns were apples in a bowl. Their curled leaves joined hands over the tablecloth. The dark holes of her eyes were picked out by a hunting knife, as if they were pellets her father took from birds. Around her neck, she had the white yoke of her old dress like a rim of milk.

Then Flutie sat at the kitchen table with her father talking clearly as if she never dreamed.

"Why don't you hunt deer?" Flutie asked him.

"Nothing to hunt for," he answered. "Your mother don't like deer meat, and Frank's in String-town."

35.

Flutie was seventeen and she thought of what she could do. She talked to Ruther in the Rutherford's backyard. She knew she had to speak if she wanted to get through school. If she wanted to go to school in Weatherford. She could hardly think about it. The words hit her head. *Southwestern Oklahoma*

State University. It was in Weatherford on Highway 183, south past Taloga. Maybe eighty miles. It made Flutie small. It felt like lightning struck. It was a fear that burned.

"See all the clouds? All the birds lined up on the telephone wire? Talk in front of them," Ruther said. "This's a crowded place. You'll get used to it."

Flutie looked at the sky.

There was a deer who wove a story with its hooves. See how the leaves clumped together, she said.

36.

Juke Box Blues. The bar and dance hall in Woodward. Sometimes Flutie went with Swallow, and they stayed overnight at her sister's. Sometimes she went with Geneva, Franklin's wife, who was living in Franklin's room while he was at Stringtown. Sometimes she drove with Jess. "Marry me, Flutie," he said. If she drank enough, she could go by herself. Juke box blues is what Flutie had. She liked the thought.

The blue light from the juke box made Jess' eyes look milky, but when he turned away, they were dark again and small. Almost lost in his head. The room danced with cowboy songs.

Flutie's mother was out driving the highways. Sometimes to Stringtown and back. Her father buried himself under cars at the Hampton's Garage. Flutie could do what she wanted.

She felt another world moving through the roof. Now it was alcohol that protected her. Alcohol was the field she ran into. When she woke in the morning she'd be shaky. She'd feel uncovered, like a deer without its skin. Flutie had the skin of both worlds. She was half her father's Indian culture, half her mother's white culture, but she walked in none. Maybe the branches could stick their leaves onto her and she'd be a tree. A tree couldn't speak like a deer.

She was going to take the music and dance up to heaven with it. She was going to slip right off the earth. She could see where the sparkles from her thoughts and prayers were. Once when she'd sat in Ruther's chaise lounge and looked into the sky, she could see a hundred sparks. A thousand. The Baptist minister could take his high water gospel at church and speak it into being. She would decide for herself what it said.

Flutie sat by the window in Juke Box Blues and looked out into the street. Maybe someone would come and take her away.

37.

In class Flutie wanted to say her last name was Moses. Her father's father had gone to boarding school, and whatever his name had been, it became Moses. Maybe it was her father's grandfather who'd been given a new name, who'd stood on the new land of Oklahoma when it became a state in 1907, and had its name changed from Indian Territory. But Oklahoma still meant *Red Man's Land*.

Why didn't her father ever tell her what she wanted to know? *Because it wasn't worth anything,* Flutie's mother said later as she tore across the road.

The waves washed over Flutie, spotted with cattle swimming in the sea.

38.

Once there'd been an icestorm and the schoolbus had gone off the road. Beatrix, the driver, had been in trouble and Flutie was the only one who'd seen what happened. Swallow was talking to someone, and no one but Flutie and the driver had seen the coyote that ran across the road. The schoolbus had swerved and gone into the ditch. No one was hurt, but the fender was dented and the parents worried when their children were late.

It was Flutie's father in the tow truck from Hampton's Garage that pulled the bus from the ditch, working until nearly dark with the children shivering by the road.

Flutie had stood before the school principal and said that it wasn't Beatrix's fault. She'd done what she could.

Yes, once Flutie had talked. She'd been Philomela holding her tongue in her hand. Only Flutie had thrown her tongue in the pond. It had swam.

39.

Flutie's mother had to go to court in Woodward. Flutie's father went with her. When she came back she tore the house up. She was not allowed to drive. *Who were they to do that?* She yelled.

"You got a string of tickets," her father yelled back.

If she wanted to go anywhere, Geneva or Flutie or Flutie's father would drive her. Or Franklin when he came back from Stringtown. If he could stay out of trouble.

"You're slower than the wheat growing," Flutie's mother glared at her. "I'm not riding with you."

40.

Strange images came into Flutie's head. Ghosts of old cattle herds that passed through the land. The barren field of the salt plains near Jet, further to the northeast. Maybe there was some hidden Oklahoma quicksand. The juke box records twirling in her eyes like pools of oil. Their puddles swirling on the land. Where was the oil money from all the oil pumps on the land? None of the farmers ever saw it. Flutie listened to Geneva talk after supper. The air sometimes whistled in her teeth. Flutie would use the money to go to school. If only she could speak.

It all turned in a box bordered with neon lights. It was all lost on hope. In the cafe, when the men said the bottom fell out of the oil market and the rigs would shut down, Vini went on as it always had.

41.

Late Saturday morning when Flutie woke in her own room she wondered how she got here. Maybe the man had dumped her off and she had crawled into the house. Maybe the spirits. They'd been known to do that. Once when she was chasing after her brother with a knife, the spirits had yanked the knife backward out of her hand, slicing the fan of skin between her thumb and finger.

Everything seemed to come in pieces.

Her mother was yelling at her to get a job. They needed the money. Geneva worked in Woodward, in City Hall, in the land deed and records office. She paid her way.

Flutie's mother was upset that Franklin was restless in Stringtown. The last time Flutie drove her there, he cried in frustration. He hit the wire window between them in rage. The guards had taken Franklin back to his cell while her mother yelled at them.

Flutie felt queazy.

Franklin, Flutie cried in her room. She wanted to be a deer for him. Put him on her back. Tell him to hold onto her antlers. Take him out of Stringtown. Out of Vini. Give him something to do. Give him hope.

She wanted to take him to school. Erase his frustration. His inability to read. She wanted to turn the letters in his school books into words, into sentences, into thoughts, into understanding of what was said on the pages.

Franklin's story would consume her. She felt it wrapping her with string as she cried for him. She had to pull away.

Franklin knew no release but a custom car on the road. He and his black leather friends had made their own angry world to live in.

*　　*　　*

Flutie still dreamed of a white duck running into the room, saying, *chop shop, chop shop*. It had taken twenty-five stitches to close her wounds.

Her mother had raced her to Woodward. They'd wrapped her in a sheet and held her down.

Flutie was stuck, and the more she tried to move, the more she moved down. She could see deeper in the earth, through the bedrock, into the earth's molten engine room. Some mornings she tasted lava.

Flutie asked Jess to take her to the cemetery to find her father's mother's grave.

"The scar travels upward on your face," Jess said as they walked through the short, stiff grass, "as if a wing had been there. As if a wing were torn off."

Flutie thought she would hear a story, but there was only silence there.

Her grandmother must have taken her stories with her.

Flutie's words could have flown out, but they were stuck to the inside of her mouth.

If she tried to speak, the waves came from her feet, surged upward through her body. They struck her head, filling her mouth with salt water until she choked, quivering with the sting in her throat.

*　　*　　*

If the railroad still came through Vini, she could ride to the next town.

Instead, she walked into Carpter's Drygoods in Vini. She looked at Mr. Carpter behind the counter. "I want to work." She felt her legs tremble.

"What can you do?"

"I don't know." The words felt like skillets on the hot stove of her tongue.

"We got inventory the end of next month. Come back then. Can you count?"

She nodded that she could.

Outside in the air, the sparkles ran before her eyes like the glitter of angels. Now it was words she saw. The spirit beings that words caused. Baby angels. Spittle from God's tongue when he looked down at his beloved ones, lisping about how much he cared. Yet they lived in trailers and run-down farmhouses and didn't have money to buy what they needed, but lived on make-dos and I-owe-yous and next-year-we'll-get-aheads. The truth of it never was. They shifted in their chairs at the supper table and shared their bread and gravy.

On the wings of music and alcohol Flutie could fly. The cowboy bars and dance halls on the two-lane highway from Gotebo to Seiling to Taloga to Vini to Woodward. She lived with the nightflyers and bats and whatever passed before the headlights. It was under a blanket of beer she rose to herself. Higher than she'd been in the back row of church where the windows above seemed to twinkle like the Oklahoma land under the sun, and the cattle grazed the heatwaves. She went to church with Jess sometimes. It was God's word and the beer that could raise her from her seat.

Sometimes she looked down the highway and saw it like a corridor into space. Somewhere there was a house, up there in the sky. She thought she could almost see it. Jesus was sitting on a chair. It was a music hall, something she hadn't seen before, a great hall with balconies, with stories and stories of heaven. Up and up it went, full of people who had ever lived. All of them speaking. Maybe it was there that she could speak. In the afterlife, way down the road. But she rode with Jess rolling over the road, the way he did sometimes with his arm around her, the way men drove when they were drunk.

Before they knew it, they'd slip into the sky.

It was words like dust she saw floating in the air. She stuck her tongue out. Maybe they'd come from the other way. Outward in. But a dry wind caught in her throat and she coughed.

42.

"Maybe you shouldn't leave your mouth open so long." Somehow Franklin was there in the morning.

Flutie moved in the kitchen like a hatchet. Maybe she'd known he was coming back from Stringtown and just forgot. Flutie had none of her father's grace. Or her mother's swiftness. Or her brother's sluggardliness.

We're still here. Flutie's father shook his head. He never spoke his feelings, but he was father of the children and husband of the mother, and he would sit in the kitchen before he went to work in Hampton's Garage. What else was there?

Franklin dumped his duffel bag in the kitchen and went upstairs to Geneva. Flutie and her father ate breakfast while they heard the love they made. Flutie's mother stood in the yard until they finished.

When Franklin came back down, he drove off in the truck.

43.

Flutie talked Jess into driving west on Highway 60 to Texas. Jess didn't want to go, but he wanted to be with Flutie.

In the distance, to the south, she saw the Antelope Hills. She'd seen their marks on a map in a book she read at school. The marks were two circles of parallel lines as if a child's small drawing of the sun. Only the Antelope Hills were two suns on the map. Buttes or mesas. What was the difference? Flutie wanted to study the earth. She wanted to know the names of its parts. She wanted to study the rocks she found and wrapped with string.

Flutie and Jess stopped at the Branding Iron Lounge in Arnett, the town west of Vini, the only town between Vini and the Texas border. Then they walked around the square. The Long Horn Bar on the other side. The usual. A pool table. Neon beer signs. Bar stools. Darkness that made Flutie's eyes sting in the bright light again. They drove on toward Texas.

At the border, there was a stone monument that said, *Texas*. The fields went on. Much the same. There wasn't any difference.

"Satisfied?" Jess asked.

They stopped at the Rebel Cafe and Club on the Oklahoma side of the border, where the low sun burned like an electric disk at the window.

On the way back to Vini, they passed through Arnett again, this time without stopping, because they were high on beer. Flutie read, "Circle Motel and RV. What's RV?" Flutie asked.

"Return to Vini," Jess answered.

Flutie watched the Antelope Hills in the distance. She saw Texas Gulf Refining Company with its towers as they passed.

"Looks like a launching site," Flutie said.

The only other company on the highway was the Salt Water Disposal.

"Marry me, Flutie," Jess always said.

Then in the distance, Flutie could see the granary silos in Vini like a great white ship in the dusk.

44.

At the Juke Box Blues, Flutie went blind for a moment. Pot. Weed. Reefer. Shrooms washed down by beer. Flowering on the floor of the sky. Flutie felt a buzzy high, a sleepy laughter. Some of Franklin's friends were strafing her. They were laughing. She had to get away.

45.

Flutie felt sick. Her stomach churned. She had pain above her eye that traveled through her head. Each stab made another wave of nausea. She knew how Franklin felt the times he had stayed in his room until noon. Her stomach flowed to her mouth. She talked to the corners of her bed. She talked to the heat in her attic room. To Jesus on the wall. He seemed to turn into a spirit being with braids and a disk of light behind his head. No, he was Jesus. There was someone else. A spirit being. She also walked in and out of Flutie's head as if Flutie had no skull, and her hair was curtains that opened and closed with the breeze of her passing.

Flutie saw her jeans and tee shirts on their hooks. The thought of putting them on made her body quiver. Her old dress had hanged there too, but Flutie's mother had given it to the Baptist Church.

Flutie still heard the juke box play. She felt like she rode with her mother when she was stuck behind a truck. Or a harvester or harrow. Sometimes a large truck came from the other way, and Flutie's mother passed it on a narrow bridge. It made the flowing rise. Flutie vomited into a towel. She only wanted to think of when she didn't hurt anymore.

Jess leaned by her bed. "Hold on, Flutie." He was the one who held the towel.

Her mother yelled up the stairs.

"She's sick, Mrs. Moses." Jess' voice was loud. The pain jabbed Flutie's head.

Later Flutie woke again. Maybe she'd heard Franklin and her father starting to argue. She listened, but the house was quiet. Flutie's hair was stuck to her face. She saw a girl through the window. Smaller than she should have been. She was standing in the tree in the yard, leading a bear, an elk, a moose, and a deer. A hat like the full moon behind her head. How did the moon stay without falling off? The girl was the spirit being Flutie had seen.

Now the small girl was in the room. She wasn't a girl. She was fully grown. "What do you want?" she asked Flutie, the reins for the animals still in her hand.

"I want to die. I want my death to be a driving. My hands on the wheel, my foot pushing down."

The spirit had pigtails and beaded shoes. She wore jeans, but they were embroidered. Over her jeans, she wore a skirt, russet as the Oklahoma soil. Over the skirt, she wore a shorter dress. Flowers grew from her feet. A disk of light flew at her head like a flag.

46.

"I'll give you a story, Flutie," her father said. "You can't drink. It's a suckhole you get in and can't get out. Half our Indian people are in that hole. No, more than half. You go there, you won't come back."

Flutie stood near him as he worked. Franklin stayed away from the garage when he returned from Stringtown.

"What are you doing to the Ford?" Flutie asked, leaning on the fender with a trembling hand.

"I'm selling the Ford."

"What?" Flutie didn't want her father to sell the car. A wave of nausea weakened her legs. She ran from the garage and vomited near the barrels and trellis of primrose. A smell of stale beer sickened her again.

Flutie looked at the sky over the garage. Sometimes on the prairie she could feel the earth drive through space, leaving a wake of dust. Sometimes her hangovers had a speed of their own.

"Why're you selling the Ford?" Flutie asked when she went back in the garage.

"A person can't hold on to anything. Everything's on a migration trail."

"Why?"

"It just is. Maybe to stay alive."

She saw the grille of the Ford her father polished. It looked like shark teeth.

Flutie sat behind the garage and looked at the sky. She listened to the hum of wind in the electricity wires, the telephone wires, the fences. Her days floated over her like clouds passing nowhere. What was the name of heaven? What had the Baptist minister called it? A dome? *Rackah?* No, Flutie was thinking of Ruther's rack of heaven. For the minister, heaven was closed off by a dome. Or maybe the dome was there to keep them inside heaven, so they didn't fall into outer space. But Ruther had made a rack of the minister's metal dome. Above the few clouds, beyond the blue space, was the rack of heaven like a farmer's cattleguard. Sometimes when Flutie drank, she could feel the rungs under her feet. Sometimes when she drank she could feel the sorrow in her house. The arguing she heard was an expanding universe.

47.

"You got to forgive Franklin," Flutie said to her father. "Otherwise the house has knives for walls. It has knives for tables and chairs."

Was it her father there? Was she imagining? She couldn't be sure. Jess had brought her home. He'd found her stumbling on Highway 34 from Woodward. Someone had slapped her. Her mother? Someone had tried to get her up the stairs. She thought it was her father. She weighed as much as the granary silo in Vini as he pulled her to her room.

"Tell Frank it's okay," she thought she was saying to her father.

"You can't drink anymore, Flutie," her father said. He told her a story as she wretched in the backyard. "My words are stones you have to walk on. Otherwise, you're going to fall into a black pit."

48.

Flutie worked in back of Carpter's Drygoods taking inventory. It wasn't anything that Mr. Carpter couldn't have done himself.

Flutie was too awkward to be a waitress in the Green Cafe. She'd drop the mashed potatoes all over the customers and run crying from the cafe. She'd forget the orders. She wouldn't be able to stand up to the customers. It took Swallow to do that. Swallow could skate through the all-you-can-eat-Friday-night-catfish-fries. All she had to do was look at the customers and they threw tips at her. Franklin was one of them, after he came back from Stringtown, while Geneva worked in Woodward. But Flutie could stand naked in the Green Cafe, and all they'd notice would be her shaking knees.

Someday someone would ride into town and say, *get in my car, Flutie, we're going out of here. We're going.* And Flutie would ride away. Past Gotebo, Oklahoma City, the first rest station in space. That's what she wanted. The interstate to Texas. Or New Mexico farther west. Albuquerque. The sky.

Someday someone would ask her.

49.

Flutie looked at the cars as she walked with her father through the car show in Oklahoma City where he'd come to sell the '42 Ford coupe. She stopped at a booth. *Your hand-print preserved in wax.*

She saw the man from Dennis Welding between Woodward and Vini. She saw another man walk past as she stood there. He smiled at her. He was a little heavy, but she'd go with him. If it weren't for his pants hanging too low in back. If it weren't for his 3-inch chop.

Flutie saw her father talking to a man. She knew her father was selling the Ford. She didn't know who the man was. She didn't want to know where the Ford was going.

Later that night, Flutie rode back to Vini with her father, who was silent as he drove. She looked at the road behind her, the Florentine blue 1942 Ford Super DeLuxe sedan coupe no longer on the trailer behind her father's truck. The trailer rattling as if it were the hand of the old sea still slapping the land.

50.

Veni. Vidi. Vici. I came. I saw. I conquered. Well, she'd seen the land. She'd seen the horizon, and the sky spreading itself all over the land. Nothing but the wandering cemetery pines to hold it back. She felt the sky on her sometimes. She'd brush it like a cobweb or something that flew in the window from the air.

Flutie drove the truck and cried as she drove. Her mother had pushed her out of the house to look for work.

She had to speak a road into being, but the words would not come. Maybe someday they would. Language was the mechanic that would take her away.

She turned into a drive. They were newcomers. No one knew where they came from. They were probably a family who drifted from place to place, leaving unpaid bills and a burnt-out house trailer behind them. That was the story. Just set fire to it to clean up the mess. Saved them doing the dishes and making the bed.

Flutie left her name in case they wanted someone to watch their kids. The little brats stood looking at her as she backed the truck out of their drive.

51.

She could fish in the pond on Jess' place and not catch anything. She could think of the salt-water sea as they rowed the boat. But the pond was small and they were at the shore before she could finish day-dreaming. It was the ocean shore in Oklahoma. She thought of the fish that swam there. Once she and Jess dug bones out of the soil. *Prehistoric fish bones,* Jess said.

"Southwestern Oklahoma State University in Weatherford would like to know about them."

"You're always thinking about someplace else," Jess said.

Flutie kept a bone in her room. She kept it in the box with deer-hide scraps and rocks she'd wrapped with string. The old ocean beat the shore at night. Flutie could feel it in her bed. It rolled in and out of her attic room. Maybe it had something to do with the ghost tribe that was near the pond. Maybe it was just Franklin and Geneva in Franklin's room. But more often now, they fought instead of loved.

52.

"What would you have if you wanted?" Ruther asked.

"I want to speak."

"You can do it."

"No, I can't," Flutie told her.

In school she refused to speak. She refused to give her final report in science class. The teacher threatened her with failure. The class was silent as she stood in front of everyone with the underwater volcano she'd made. She wanted to say, *Submarine volcano cones form on the ocean floor like dust balls under your bed.* If she could begin at the beginning and not have to jump in half way. But she'd shortened her report to get through it quicker. Now she didn't know where she was.

> *The viscous lava rising through volcanic vents*
> *seawater seeping down*
> *molten rock and violent steam blasts*

erupt large amounts of steam and ash
from the water into the air.

Flutie tried to make a billow with her hands. They shook like one of the violent steam blasts.

Erupting on the sea floor
from pillow-like masses.

She could rest her head on her volcano cone if it were night. She could fall into sleep and forget her science report. She stood in front of the room saying nothing. She looked at her feet until the tears blurred her eyes.

She had worked at the kitchen table on her papier-mâché underwater volcano. Taking old newspapers from the Green Cafe, tearing them into strips, mixing them with flour and glue and water, shaping her volcano cone, painting it with tan shoe polish when it dried. It's something she'd wanted to do since grade school, but she never thought she could. The kitchen would never be the same. But she had finished her volcano for the report.

But Flutie couldn't speak. No matter how many underwater volcanoes she made. She felt her cheeks flush.

Franklin had watched her make the volcano. "Why don't you just use a cow patty?" he asked.

53.

Now Flutie didn't know if she would graduate. She cried after school and wouldn't tell her mother what was wrong.

Her mother yelled at her, tore at her hair. Flutie sobbed that she couldn't talk in front of class, that the science teacher would not let her pass.

Flutie's mother sped down the dirt road.

When she came back, she flung a graduation robe at Flutie who was stirring potatoes on the stove.

54.

It was over a hundred. The air conditioning in the gymnasium didn't work. Graduation would be held in the field. Some of the girls fainted.

The evening was hot as her father's sweat lodge. It was hot as the words he yelled at Franklin who yelled back that he didn't want to go to Flutie's graduation.

"You're going to see what you couldn't do," her father said. "You're going to see someone who didn't fail."

Flutie thought she could hear their words as the principal handed her a diploma. Would her family fight in the bleachers in front of everyone? *Just get the Moseses out of here,* the teachers probably thought.

55.

Flutie pumped gas at Hampton's Garage when Franklin and her father were busy. She rode to Woodward with Geneva, but she still couldn't find work. Out of nothing else to do, she told her mother she wanted to go to Southwestern Oklahoma State University in Weatherford. Franklin laughed. There was a scholarship for students with Indian blood, but Flutie didn't have a card. *She'd pay her parents back,* she said, before she knew what she said. Flutie realized they didn't have money. But maybe they could get it. She didn't know how. For some reason, Flutie's mother wanted her to go to school, though she told Flutie her grades were poor. But she talked Flutie's father into it. Maybe she had wanted to go herself. *Ist ja wieder gut.* They'd borrow tuition from the bank.

56.

Her father didn't see the speed bump in the street, and tossed their heads against the roof of the truck. "That's more like something you'd do," he said to Flutie's mother. When they passed the First United Methodist Church on campus, Flutie saw the cross and red flame. There was an underwater volcano in Weatherford too, Flutie thought.

At the next *dip* sign, Flutie's father slowed.

She could still smell the sour smell of the milk she had spilled in her father's truck. It reminded her of the smell of the Salt Plains near Jet, Oklahoma. The white sea of spilled milk.

They circled the campus once more, passing the Bulldogs' stadium, and entered the grounds from Custer Street. The Administration Building stood at the top of the hill like the throne of God. The cars parked with their noses to the curb.

Flutie and her parents went into the Administration Building. They felt awkward. It was Flutie's fault they were there. A woman behind the counter handed them the enrollment booklet and a map of the campus.

They didn't know what else to do, so they

walked. Flutie saw a little rock house standing by itself beside the Chemistry and Science Building.

Across College Street, she saw the Baptist Student Union.

As they crossed the street, Flutie looked at the students. She saw a girl who had a bookbag the same purple as the car she'd just parked. She saw a truck with a lariat hanging from the rear view mirror. She saw a license plate with a girl's name on it.

Flutie and her parents ate in the Student Union without speaking. In the upstairs restroom, there was a full-length mirror where Flutie saw herself. She looked hunched over, ready to run.

Flutie's father bought her a bookbag in the Union. He was as out of place there as she was.

Afterwards, Flutie stood on the curb by her dormitory as they drove away.

57.

The wood door of the Al Harris Library opened like a rodeo chute. The library was a bull she couldn't ride. How could she, with a father who wouldn't tell her stories, a mother who could do seventy through a small highway town, and a brother whose room was filled with license plates, hood ornaments, stolen road signs, and who'd been in Stringtown.

Flutie saw the wall of large books. The tables upstairs. All the students knowing where to go and what to do. She felt dizzy. She was the only one getting thrown.

58.

Flutie walked past the trailer park to the water tower on the hill at the top of 7th Street in Weatherford. It wasn't like Vini's water tank, which stood off the ground on long legs, but a massive barrel squatting on the hill. She could see the pasture fence and the redbrown prairie running northwest from Weatherford back to Vini. Flutie could smell the hay. She could smell the distance. She saw the weeds hitting the barbed wire fence.

Franklin would say the water tower was a space ship.

Warning buried cable, she read, and felt the wind pass over her.

She walked past the Utopia Apartments and returned to campus.

59·

Flutie wanted to say something. She was in class and something needed to be said, but she knew if she spoke she'd feel the water. The closer she came to speaking, the more agitated she became. It was like an underwater volcano erupting after building up for years. She could feel the lava boiling in her throat.

Before she knew it, she was on Highway 183, hitchhiking back to Vini, her bookbag with everything in it thrown over her shoulder.

Flutie wanted to live someplace far away. She tried to think of a place. West of Vini was the Antelope Hills. She wanted the remoteness of them.

60.

Flutie walked to the Rutherfords' and stood at the mailbox.

"The door's open when you want to come in." Ruther waved from the front door. Luther had the mower running in the backyard, and she had to yell to Flutie.

"You back early?" she asked when Flutie came in the house.

Flutie didn't answer.

Soon Luther came in from mowing, his goggles still over his eyes.

"Just let her set there, Luther," Ruther said to him.

Where else could Flutie go?

61.

Jess Tessman wanted Flutie to marry him.

What a name, her father had said.

Flutie and Jess watched the white tail of planes overhead, moving from east to west or west to east. Up there somewhere the world moved.

If she married him, she would have a house up a dirt road. They'd have to live with Jess' father at first. But then she'd have her own place. She'd fry eggs and sit with coffee. Franklin's wife Geneva would come and they'd rock their babies and talk, if they ever had babies. She'd water the flowers and wash the dishes, if she ever had flowers. She'd make the beds and bake a ham for supper and boil a few potatoes she'd taken from her mother's garden. They'd all go to car shows. No one asking her to speak. But something lodged in her throat. It was words. Not the kind that came from the outside. But those deep in her. She had something to say. But what? And who would listen? She talked to Jess about the ghosts of the land. At least, if she married Jess, and they had to live with Jess' father, they would live by the pond that glistened like God's eye. Flutie decided the pond was where the ocean had gone underground. The pond was the mouth of the aquifer. Maybe it was the cause of the oppressiveness she felt in Jess' father. Maybe it was all that sucking on him from underground. Something chilled Flutie when she thought of marrying Jess.

Before long, Franklin was on his second wife, Swallow, or Susan, as she tried to call herself now.

They lived in the same trailer park he'd lived in with Geneva.

Swallow baled hay in her bikini. Standing nearly naked in the field. Swallow embarrassed Flutie. Why couldn't her brother's wife get dressed? Jeans and a tee shirt in the fields. Heavy shoes in case the hay-baler ran over your foot. A hat to keep the sun off your eyes. Flutie wanted to jump off the hay wagon, rip her from the fields, put her in a sloppy dress, cover her body. Think of the men who looked at her.

It was noon when the men came in from the fields. Her father and the neighbor washed their hands at the sink, leaving dirty marks. Now Flutie had that to clean too. She served the men at the long table they'd brought into her mother's kitchen. They could eat in the yard, but the flies and gnats and load of insects would have been thick. Even inside she kept the flyswatter busy. Someone was always coming in or going out the door. She thought the flies could pass through the walls.

Swallow asked for another glass of lemonade. Why didn't she get it herself? Flutie had the men to take care of. At least she covered herself with jeans and one of Franklin's old shirts. Flutie could wear her shorts and tie her shirt up under her breasts and have the men look at her body too. How would Swallow like that?

Now Swallow was in jeans, talking to some of her friends who stopped on the road. Franklin went to get her back. She came with him silent and obedient for once. Usually she kicked up and caused a row. But she just followed him back. Flutie sitting there would never be anyone to talk to. What would she have to say? She didn't know anything. Flutie and Swallow weren't in the same galaxy.

It was hard to find jeans that fit.

How'd you do it, Swallow? Flutie wanted to ask.

62.

Now Flutie had a job. She drove a van full of boxes from town to town filling large yellow cardboard schoolbus displays with Nabisco crackers. She drove the van from grocery store to grocery store. "What a lamb," Franklin said. He and her father laughed at her. In the heat the van smelled like Ruther's oven. She remembered the yeasty smell of muslin curtains when she'd put her nose into them. Why was she smelling curtains? Had she been standing at the window? Wanting out of the earth?

Saltines. Cheddars. Wheat Thins. Triscuits. Honey Grahams. Oatmeal Crunch. Fig Newtons. Gingers. Pretzels. Oreos. Oat Crackers. Wheat Crackers.

She felt the wheel of the Nabisco van in her hand. She didn't have to sell. The selling had been done. She had to refill the racks. Keep them in stock. Deliver. Dust. Rearrange. Stack. Yes, and maybe once in a while stop by a store where they didn't carry Nabisco. Ask them to.

The boxes of crackers in the hot van smelled like the road. The wet garden after a downpour. The cellar. The earth.

She put her foot to the gas and the county sheriff was there. After three tickets she was fired. She was on her way to Woodward to return the van when a car turned onto the highway from a dirt road. She couldn't stop in time. To keep from hitting the car, she ran the van into the ditch and hit a fence post. It wasn't her fault. She tried to tell her boss.

Jess and Ruther sat with her in court in Woodward. The lawyer asked her what had happened. She looked down at her feet. She said words, but they stayed in a puddle on her tongue. She was talking, but she was shaking. She wasn't going anywhere. Why couldn't she stand in front of the judge like she had the school principal when Beatrix had run off the road?

Even Ruther wasn't able to speak for her.

The judge decided that the company owned the van and they would have to pay for the repairs. Then he fined Flutie $100 and took her license for a month. But she didn't have to pay for the van.

Jess would get the money from his father.

He walked out of the courtroom ahead of her.

63.

Now it was Flutie's nineteenth birthday. She sat in the Green Cafe with her family. Fried chicken and mashed potatoes with gravy. Green beans and a roll. Sounded familiar. Swallow wrapped her leg around Franklin's, and he smiled at her. Flutie knew they held hands under the table.

Flutie leaned over the cake when Swallow and

Franklin brought it from the kitchen. Flutie blew out
the candles. They came back on. She blew again.
They lit again. Franklin laughed. Jess smiled. Why
was she supposed to laugh at their joke? Their trick
candles?

Swallow didn't want a piece of Flutie's cake and
turned to Franklin. "*Wantto do, Honey?*"

"*YeahIdo.*" Franklin was agreeable as they talked.
"I gotto get over to Woodward before nightfall,"
he told them. "I got to get the lumber and hardware to build that shed. The woodfence is getting
loose."

"I want to see my sister," Swallow said. "I'd like
a blueflowered dress and a turn in the dancehall."

"I like to see you floating like I did last summer
when you caught my eye," Franklin told her with a
hug.

Flutie looked at the ceiling and thought that if
it were a dancefloor, she could crawl up the wall.
How did the flies stand on the ceiling when the door
was left open, rushing in from the night as if the
fly-swatter couldn't pancake them against the ceiling?

"You can't win against them," Swallow said.
"They won every election except the governor."

It was a *zoon* to hear them packing. What could they do? Sell water from a tank until it paid for itself. Franklin was always scheming. He was going to buy Hampton's Garage. He was going to build them a house. For now, he was taking Swallow to Woodward for the night.

64.

Flutie rode to the Baptist Church with Jess without speaking. His father made her sell eggs and clean the chicken house to pay back the $100 traffic fine. The housework and cooking she did for them didn't count. She felt she couldn't go anywhere without Jess. Weren't they almost married? Weren't they talking to the preacher about a ceremony?

"Where else you got to go?" Jess asked.

Flutie had nearly paid the bank what her family borrowed for her short stay in Weatherford. Southwestern Oklahoma State University had returned some of the tuition. If she still had her Nabisco job, it would be over.

"He walks the racks of the oven with us," Ruther said.

Flutie listened to the Baptist minister. "I sought the Lord, and he heard me, and delivered me from all my fears. Psalm 34:4."

65.

"I don't want to marry Jess."

"Get your belongings from the attic room," Flutie's mother told her. "He's comin' for you."

"What's wrong?" her father asked.

"I just don't want to live with them."

Flutie's mother laughed. "It's too late. The minister's waiting at the church."

"Franklin and Swallow live in the trailer park now. You got room," Flutie said.

Flutie's mother threw a cardboard box at her.

"It'll feel like I'm all tied up," Flutie said.

She carried the box upstairs and threw her picture of Jesus into it. Her box of rocks and salt crystals and scraps of deer-hide and the prehistoric fish bone. But she smashed the papier-mâché volcano against the wall.

"I can't marry you, Jess," Flutie handed him the box as she came down the stairs. "I can't."

He opened the backdoor for her.

"Just leave without me," Flutie said.

"Get in the truck," Jess told her.

"No," Flutie answered, and walked through the yard toward the field.

He came after her, pulled her arm. She jerked away from him and ran.

She heard Jess calling after her.

"You ain't comin' back," her mother yelled. "You just live with the deer."

Flutie heard Jess tear down the road in a flush of gravel as she crossed the field.

She would keep walking and wouldn't stop until she reached Ruther's.

Flutie slept on a withered sofa for a night, but Luther's breathing woke her several times. She felt Ruther's spirits flying through the room, tripping in the hall, their hair quivering with heat.

For a few nights, Flutie slept in Ruther's shed with Luther's mower and the night animals. She heard them come and go in the shed, gnawing on something. Their speech reduced to a few grunts in the silence that would consume her until she was more afraid of the silence than she was the speaking.

She couldn't be quiet. She knew it. She'd been quiet all her life. It was a hole blacker than the shed. She had to talk. The land talked. The past talked. All that was to come talked. Already she could hear it. She would mimic the talking she heard. She would be a part. She would speak even if it shook her bones. She would speak even if her throat closed and she suffocated on the words. Even if she choked on the salt she always tasted. Even if she were painted red with shame and hanged on the flagpole at school.

Not speaking was a wall before her. She couldn't climb it. She knew her failure. She would be locked in it forever. The thought burned her head. No. She couldn't stand to be shut up in silence. She would walk into the speaking. If it knocked her flat, she would get up. The dust would unfold like a tongue. She said she would speak, though she didn't believe it in her head. She said it the way Ruther talked the rain *hither*. If she didn't speak, the rocks would speak for her. Isn't that what the gospels said? It was one of the things she remembered the Baptist minister saying.

"Luke 19:40." She asked Ruther who looked it up in the Bible.

*   *   *

One morning she walked down the road to her house and up the stairs into the attic room with the smashed volcano still on the floor.

66.

Flutie felt she was so far away that no one could ever find her. They could fish for years. But she was tired of the silence. She was going to speak. She said her name, *Flutie. Flutie Moses.* She said her story.

A deer came from the water. He was a rusted submarine with four legs. One antler like a periscope.

The birds on the telephone wire laughed.

No.

Flutie started again. *A deer came from the water. She was brown. She had no tongue.*

"I want to go to school again," Flutie told Ruther in her backyard.

"Then go," Ruther said. The dust from the mower blew across their laps.

Flutie put her fingers in her ears so she wouldn't hear Luther's noise.

A deer came from the air, Flutie said.

She watched a dog cross the field in the stillness that stirred up the grasshoppers. She was scared. There was someone pushing her away. Maybe it was the ghosts. But how could she go back to Weatherford? She didn't have money. She didn't want to live with Jess and his father. She couldn't live with her parents. Nor Swal and Franklin.

She wouldn't want to.

They wouldn't want her.

"I want to study geology, Ruther," Flutie said another day.

"Go talk to the bank," Ruther answered. "Ask Turbo again."

The loan officer's name was Bill Smith, but Ruther called him Turbo because he was slow.

The first time Flutie'd gone to Weatherford, she had sat in his office shaking. He'd been kind and had given her a loan. Why did she still want to run? Why did she always feel she was wrapped in a sheet?

Turbo Smith gave Flutie another loan. On the wall, she saw his accounting degree from Southwestern State. There was something about a call from Ruther. Something about collateral.

Flutie would return to Weatherford.

She sat in her room wrapping a rock with string.

67.

It was Flutie's turn to work through an algebra problem on the board. In speaking, Flutie felt the storm hit. The water pounded her head. She felt her unsteady knees. She knew she may not survive, but she was going to speak.

The Great Spirit reached down and poked her throat open and let out the lava. She was in the power of her voice. She spoke the boiling words. Her whole being rocked. Her head spasmed. She sat down. The room shook with her. But it was done.

That night under the thin spread of her dormitory bed, she saw the shadowy hole in the darkness in her head. The Elders looking down. The hole was like an open mouth. It said SHE HAD A MOUTH THAT OPENED TO SPEAK. She looked again at the shadowy hole. Now it looked like the disk behind the spirit being's head. Now it looked like an open mouth. The elders were its teeth. Her words had been snarled up inside her. It seemed they'd never get out. But she remembered she had spoken. She had walked by herself through the wet leaves as a deer.

She would sit in all her classrooms feeling she made the other students uncomfortable. When she spoke her words came through the floor of the ocean. They would like to be without that. How little anyone wanted her.

Trembling, she had to speak in another class. Would it always toss her like an ocean? Flutie stood in front of the room. *I open my mouth. I am a deer. My deer in the water swims for the air.* Flutie breathed in the light. She would hold onto her words like she'd held to that old plaid dress she'd wanted in the second-hand store in Woodward. The light from the windows made a glare in the classroom. She thought she heard a powersaw cutting the waves. HIGH and HOLY SPIRIT, she could almost hear Ruther say. Look up from underwater. Look through the hole the saw cut. She could see the sky!

She traveled in her head all that day. She would speak in the next class and the next. Tongues would fill her mouth. Soon she wouldn't be able to wait for her turn.

Flutie saw the smoke detector blinking from the ceiling like a lighthouse. Yes, she was out on the dark waters, but she was rowing as if nearing land. Little by little she would speak.

Women had tongues that went into the water. They could taste the lava between the cracks of bedrock on the ocean floor. They forgot sometimes in the day. But at night, in the dark, they could feel their tongues reaching.

In the hall, Flutie kept her eyes on the red blinking light. It was on the shore. Yes. If she kept rowing she'd make it.

Onward.

Onward.

She rowed to the land.

68.

Well, it wasn't that easy. Flutie had to speak in class again. The same fear came back. This time Flutie thought of the land. The soil was rusted as if it had been kissed by the salt air of the old sea. She thought of cattle in a field. A house without paint. An abandoned car in a gulley. The car was rusting as if the red soil had kissed it also, leaving its stain. No, Flutie decided the car was not the make Franklin would want. He was always scouring western Oklahoma. Maybe he'd even been to Texas. He didn't need her help.

Flutie went over and over the land in her mind while she waited for her turn.

Telephone lines. Posted warnings. Dirt roads that spread out into the country. Risely Farm. Oil pumps and storage tanks. Red ponds stained red as the soil.

She couldn't go back to Jess, she told herself.

She couldn't live on the land behind Vini, up a long dirt road where no one would ever find her.

69.

In the music room, Flutie saw the notes on the staves across the pages. How could the marks cause such sound? They were deer hoofprints in a field. A deer herd. A stave of notes moving, yet she couldn't hear anything. She touched the page. There was silence. Yet the story of the music was there. It was like the tapestry Philomela wove. Someone could read it. Someone would know what to do. The hoof marks were a map that moved the fingers, that moved the keys or buttons or whatever the parts of the horns that you pushed with your fingers to make a herd of sounds. How silent the music looked as it sat opened on the stand. Just some hoofprints on a page. But Flutie had heard the music of the hooves. The notes of hoof marks arranged on the fenced field of the stanzas; some, even, with antlers that indicated *graze, walk, run, stand.*

70.

Franklin was working under a car when the jack or the hydraulic lift broke. Flutie didn't get it straight because her mother was screaming, but Swallow tried to tell her the car fell on Franklin's leg and they were afraid he'd lose it. He'd been taken to Woodward, then Oklahoma City.

71.

Flutie returned to Vini when Franklin came back on crutches. He had bottles of medicine and pills for pain, for infection, for circulation. Swallow gave him a glass of water, which he turned over, whether from awkwardness or anger.

"You get them bandages wet, you'll have to go through having your leg and foot wrapped again," Swallow said, sopping the water with a gown he brought back.

"You know Franklin," his father said, "you got the only woman in western Oklahoma who'll stay with you."

"Spare me what you think."

72.

Swallow sat at supper with her fork in her turnips. She passed the bread.

"How's my cowgirl?" Franklin asked bitterly at the table.

Flutie sat quietly at the table.

No one spoke.

"My leg will always hurt," Franklin said.

"I'll be glad to rub your foot to keep the circulation going anytime you want, Frank," Swallow said.

"Keep your foot up on the chair, Franklin. You know what the doctor said," Franklin's father said.

"Fuck the doctor."

"You have to keep the blood in your leg," Franklin's mother said.

"I could take my leg off at the garage. I could leave my foot in my boot."

Flutie was going to stay just for the weekend, but at the end of the week, she was still in her attic room with the box of her things Jess had returned.

Flutie's mother called up the stairs. Flutie's roommate was on the phone. Flutie looked at her bookbag hanging on a nail, and said to tell her roommate she'd be back. Jess also called. Flutie wouldn't talk to him either.

73.

Flutie returned from the grocer with some beans and lamb. She stirred the stew while Swallow sat in the backyard with Flutie's mother's old shawl over her lap.

Swallow was restless. From the kitchen Flutie could see the way her foot jerked under the shawl.

Flutie's mother was shelling walnuts Mr. Carpter gave Flutie. Flutie knew her mother could see Swallow from the window.

"Is Franklin sleeping?" Flutie asked when Swallow came in.

"For a moment. I can't stay here, Flutie, " she said. "I have to go back to our trailer." Swallow hadn't seen Flutie's mother sitting at the table. She sat down with her.

Flutie cooked supper while her mother finished the walnuts and Swallow rested her head on the table, wiping her nose from time to time. Then Flutie's father was back from the garage and walked Frank to the kitchen on his crutches.

Franklin ate, sopping the lamb stew gravy with his bread.

"He'll get better, Swal," Flutie said as they

washed dishes. "He hates for you to see him this way," but Swallow had gone out like a light in the next farmhouse at night.

74.

That night the yard light didn't come on. Flutie got the flashlight and found the kerosene lamp from the pantry and filled the glass bowl because she didn't want the dark. The wax candles Flutie's mother also kept in case of storms and no electricity, stained the drawer like oil had stained the garage.

The light flickered. "You pay the light bill, Flutie?" her father asked.

"I was thinking of moving Franklin's bed in the parlor or in the hallway because of the breeze," her mother said.

"Flutie?" her father kept after her.

"No, I forgot."

Flutie sat in Franklin's truck. Well, it was Swallow's now too. But Swallow didn't care. If she wasn't going somewhere with Franklin, she didn't want to go anywhere. How had Swallow fallen in love? She wanted to leave the Moseses' house. Flutie saw that.

Swallow wanted nothing more than to drive off down the road. But Swallow didn't leave. What made her stay with Franklin? Was it love? How did it happen? Why hadn't Flutie been able to feel that way with Jess? She did not want to live with him and his father. Nothing could make her want to.

The roof light in the truck was burnt out. Flutie felt for the keys. They were in the ignition. That way Frank always knew where they were. She started the truck in the dark.

Where was she going?

Over her, the stars had paid their electric bill.

She felt a sudden pull back to Weatherford. She remembered her bookbag on its nail. She returned quickly to her attic room.

She had to stay in school. What if she had to support Franklin, if he didn't take care of his leg? She blundered where the rock waited on the dark road. How hard it would be for some truck whose driver didn't know it was there.

But how could she go back to school? she thought as she headed down the dark road. "What can you do?" Franklin asked her all her life. His friends also confronted her, made fun of her. She wanted to be able to do something, but how could she do something when she'd never done anything?

How could she?

She could keep the truck on the road to Weatherford. She could walk into her room. Into her classes. She could not turn back. She could tell her feet a long story of going on.

"What the fuck did you do with my truck?" Franklin said to Flutie on the phone in Weatherford.

"I drove it back to school."

"In the middle of the night?"

"I'm not the first to drive out of the yard in the dark," Flutie said. "I had to borrow your truck. If I waited until daylight, I wouldn't have come back to school."

Franklin was quiet for a moment, then said, "You got to watch for the deer at night."

75.

Now it was summer and Flutie was back from school. She looked at Vini as she drove into town. The Green Cafe was a brick building. It had a green door, which was pale as asparagus, bleached by the

Oklahoma sun. Swallow told her the cafe had been redecorated. Flutie decided to have lunch.

Inside there were green tables and chairs, a counter and pie safe. Even the cash register was green. Just fifty miles from Texas. On the walls were dust-bowl posters of open-mouthed farmers gaping their way west. The women's auxiliary of the historical society was looking at the culture of the land. They'd decided to hang the posters in the cafe.

Flutie's mother was in driver's school. In detention. In Woodward for a few days in jail.

Swallow wanted Flutie to work in the cafe, to stay behind the counter while she ran to the garage to soothe Franklin the first few days he was back. She had to be able to leave the cafe once in a while.

Flutie stood behind the counter and watched the customers. Most of them she knew. Only once in a while someone would stop who was a stranger. Maybe Jess would come by, and would see her working there.

76.

"Shit, the gear we used on Spoon's car was less than we charged him." Franklin was looking through receipts at Hampton's Garage.

"He'll be in again," Flutie said.

"It doesn't make any difference," their mother said.

"Give him more change back next time he buys gas. It all comes out," their father said as he came in from the garage.

Flutie and her mother sat talking with them. Franklin tapped a pencil on the desk. Sometimes he said he felt like he had nothing.

"But Frank, you're back at the garage," their mother said.

"I'm not getting anywhere," he snapped as some men from Jackson's Auto Repair on Highway 34 near Woodward showed up to see him.

"That's where we're all going," one of them said.

"You got Swallow for your wife," another remarked.

"She could leave on the next train."

"There's no train stops in Vini. They only used

to pull the oil cars anyway, taking all we got some-place else."

"I can't take Franklin to the hospital. It scares me," Flutie protested the next week.

"There's no one else to take him," her mother told her.

"Just because you can't keep your foot from stomping the gas pedal."

Flutie was a coward. *White feather,* Franklin called her. *Peck. Peck,* he said, pinching her.

Flutie told her feet not to run. She stayed next to Franklin in the hospital waiting room. The doctor had to check his foot every week. Flutie trembled as she waited. It was the same fear she felt when she had to speak before a class, or before tests when she had to prove herself on the spot and knew she couldn't.

"They look like ducks in their white coats," Flutie said of the doctors who passed.

"Once someone at school dressed like Donald Duck and you screamed. He took off his duck mask but you still screamed."

"I thought he was a doctor who was going to hold me down and sew up my head."

"Quack. Quack." Franklin leaned on his crutches and poked Flutie's scars.

77.

Flutie's father's people were here on the land when her mother's people came. Some of them from the northern lakes region. Germans from Minnesota. The people who came had to get rid of those who were already here, and they'd have to make it look right.

They had a land run.

In fact, they had more than one.

"Why didn't your family leave during the dust bowl?" Flutie asked Ruther.

"I guess the family just decided to stick it out," she answered.

Flutie liked the historical posters at the Green Cafe. Sometimes she stood looking at them. Carpter had hung a few at the drygoods store and there were some at the hardware. There had also been historical articles in the newspaper.

Ruther talked to Flutie as she and Luther dug in a creekbank south of town for the remains of plates and implements used by the first white settlers in Western Oklahoma. They'd lived in sod houses and lean-tos dug into ravines. One cracked plate Ruther found was from France. She fussed at Luther in his goggles as he worked, flinging dirt past them with his shovel.

In the night, Luther's breathing woke Ruther. Flutie heard her walk down the hall from the couch where Flutie slept that night. Ruther must have thought Luther was out mowing the yard, but when she went to the window, she realized he was in his room.

Don't Resuscitate, Flutie remembered. She knew Ruther stood at Luther's door, his goggles hanging on the bedpost.

She stood there until Luther quieted.

"You were mowing in your sleep, Luther," Ruther said as she poured grits into their bowls.

"I want to be buried in my goggles."

"You been saying that for years. You're going to be here long as I am."

"No, I won't, Ruther. You're going to have some of it without me. The ancestors are crowding into them overstuffed chairs again. There's more of them all the time. Some are from far away. They talk in the hall. They stand in the kitchen with us. Some of them haven't seen each other in a while."

"Since dad's funeral, I guess," Ruther said.

"They been out traveling in space."

Flutie listened to them as she ate.

"There's a whole universe for you to mow, Luther."

"That's why I want the goggles. I thought I'd make it to the end that's coming, when the earth turns to dust. I can feel it when I mow. The end is near. Now I'm going to miss it. It's hard to let go and pass away. I'm not sure where I'm going. Or how long it'll take to get there."

78.

The car show in Oklahoma City. Franklin couldn't walk far without resting. His leg hurt, he said, even when he used the crutches. Swallow sat with him until some men looked at her and made Franklin mad. She got up and walked off, Franklin calling her back, yelling her name when she kept walking.

They were all arguing, Flutie's mother and father too. Their tempers rising in the heat. For once, just once, Flutie was glad she was quiet. She liked her quietness as she stood apart from them watching. She could be there or not be there. She didn't let herself show like them.

She could choose not to share, not to take part. She could withdraw from all the talking. She could be quiet while they yelled, and it was something like satisfaction she felt.

But maybe her quietness was because they didn't give her a chance. Maybe she would have joined them if she could. Could she yell at them to shut up? If they'd just listen. But they wouldn't hear her. Flutie withdrew into the room in her head from which no words sounded, and walked among the cars.

They were nobility. American nobility. The vintage and custom cars transcended to the highest hope of the common man. Flutie saw the men walking around them, looking. There was transformation. There was hope. Cars were the angels of America. They were full of invisible wings. Chevys.

Fords. Plymouths. Buicks. Studebakers. Restored. Rebuilt. Customized. Polished. Worshipped.

The cars were stories. They were words. Flutie thought they were the voice of God.

Some boys were gawking at the hot-rod magazine girl. One of them threw popcorn at her low-cut dress, trying to get it between her breasts. The magazine girl's chaperone told the boys to go away. Franklin pushed them with his crutch. "Get your dinkies off someplace else," he said, and they moved on. Swallow laughed, and Franklin had his arm around her again.

Flutie saw a white angel. Made to drive in heaven. Queen of the cars. A white '38 Ford with a white interior and a chrome engine that sparkled. A car like Philomela, torn up, raped with tools, rebuilt with tapestry. The air was flying around it waiting to place a halo on its roof. The spirits were slugging it out as to who could drive it first.

Flutie stood looking at the Ford until her father called her away. She felt dizzy in the heat. For a moment, she had seen a hood ornament, different from the one on the car. She had seen through some strange angle in the heat. The ornament was the spirit girl in her cape and dress. The disk like a headlight at her head. The cape dark as a black eye, no one could touch.

79.

In the fall, Luther was buried in his goggles.

"He died in his sleep," Ruther said, "dreaming of mowing the yard."

Flutie stood in the mortuary in Vini.

She stood in the cemetery west of Vini, which was full of cedars and gravestones.

The Baptist minister spoke from the middle of the Rutherford plot. "Some think we sleep in the here-after," he was saying, "or until the second coming of Christ, when everyone will wake." Flutie could see the Rutherfords lined up in their beds in heaven, floating among the clouds, maybe tied together with a string. But he, the minister, thought they were awake in heaven after they died, even before Christ came. Flutie looked at the gravestones of the Ruth-erford parents, the two children who died in child-hood, the grandparents, aunts, uncles, cousins. Luther was with them now. His mower was the sound of a motorcycle on the highway, or a souped-up car.

They stood in the cemetery and listened to the minister's words. They were like small frisbies flying past Ruther and Flutie, Flutie's parents, Franklin and Swallow, Mr. and Mrs. Smots and two of Swallow's sisters, the neighbors, Mr. Carpter, Beatrix, the post office clerk, Turbo the banker, the hardware store owner, the feed and seed man, the grocer, Jess and Mr. Tessman, several old ladies, Spoon and the custom car gang, the ancestors, the spirits with flames for hair. But the minister's words got blown back into his mouth in the Western Oklahoma wind that made their hair beat their faces, and their dresses and trousers flap around their legs. They stood before Luther's grave as if it were a hole he dug with his mower.

"I saw you drive down the road the other day, Flutie," Ruther said, as they ate lunch at the Baptist church after the funeral. "I thought you might be going back to school."

"I turned around and came back."

Ruther looked at her.

"I might go back winter semester."

"It'll take you fifteen years at your present rate. You got to separate from us, Flutie. You got your own road," she said.

"We'll miss him, Sister Rutherford," the Baptist minister said.

"Yes, who will mow the yard?" Ruther asked.

80.

In a store in Woodward, Flutie saw Geneva. Sometimes Flutie felt old, but she thought Geneva looked older. Since Flutie was nearly twenty, Geneva would be nearly thirty, seven years older, Flutie thought. Divorced with two children by another man, Geneva told Flutie she left the children with her mother when she worked.

Sometimes the years passed before Flutie could get ahold of them. It jarred her to think how old she was.

Flutie still hoped her cowboy would come and dance her to the highway, and they'd be off to some town she'd never heard of, where the jukebox glittered and the songs lifted her overhead to the sky. No, it was a mechanic she wanted.

She didn't go to the cowboy bars very often anymore, she told Geneva as they talked.

"My husband's on the road this week. We could go back to Juke Box Blues."

Flutie stayed away from drinking. Even Franklin managed to, because of their father's warnings. But once in a while, she went. She had to do something.

That night, Flutie saw how Geneva could hook a man from far away. It wasn't until they got up close that they knew she was old, and they heard the way she spoke through the spaces in her teeth.

Flutie saw how age came upon you. Danced you in a circle and left you by yourself. Not like the woman who came into the cafe long ago. Flutie longed to be like her.

But what could she do?

She could go back to Weatherford.

81.

They had revivals when the road was rough, which it always was. But Flutie's father didn't like them. Sometimes some of them had sweat lodges. Flutie's father had bent saplings in the backyard into a new frame. He covered the frame with tarp, until it looked like a small mound. He heated the rocks. Even Ruther took part.

Inside the dark and the heat, Flutie heard her voice. It was the flames of hair on the spirit Ruther saw.

Flutie heard the others, a neighbor and one of the men from Jackson's Auto Repair.

"I see you talking before people, Flutie," Ruther said. "Think of the words coming out your mouth like grain trucks driving to the Farmer's *Co-op.*"

"Like a line of custom cars on the highway, full of pistons and gaskets, cylinder heads and manifolds," Flutie said.

"I see Franklin walking without pain," his father said.

"I can't take a test either, Ruther," Flutie said, as they continued the round, talking to the rough road.

"I see the pencil in Flutie's hand—" Ruther didn't know what to say.

"—like Luther's mower in the dirt," Flutie finished.

They continued to sweat and pray in the lodge. Flutie remembered the people from far away on the earth. Ireland. India. She remembered their voices she'd heard from time to time in the wind. Maybe she'd heard them in other sweat lodge ceremonies. Maybe they came up from the earth. Or from within her head. She felt connected to them all. She wiped her sweat and listened to the earth. To the rocks.

Somewhere a jet passed overhead, maybe from Altus. Or Tinker, still farther away.

"Sometimes I still can hear the buffalo," Ruther said.

"What do they say?" Flutie asked.

"Something about french fries," Ruther's voice sounded puzzled. "They feel like they're walking on a tight-rope of french fries from the Green Cafe."

82.

When Flutie returned to school, her father gave her his truck, a '73 deer-brown Ford with cracked interior, when he got a new truck in Woodward.

As Flutie drove back to Southwestern State in Weatherford, she looked for another car for her father to work on. South of Vini, between Taloga and Weatherford, was Putnam, Arapahoe, all of Custer County. There was a salvage yard beyond Arapahoe. She pulled off to the side of the road a moment in the stifling heat. Then she drove on to *66 Auto Salvage and Used Parts.* The heat waves quavered on the road. She read the posters that trembled in the hot wind. There were one or two hulls advertised that her father might be interested in. Then she remembered she was on her way to school. She had to leave the garage behind for a while. She had to mark her way with classes of history, composition, geometry, chemistry, physics, fluid mechanics, electromagnetism, instead of salvage yards.

One night, Flutie saw a comet falling from the stars. The stars always changing places, she thought.

If they'd be there just once when she looked up. But they always moved, with the constellations for antlers.

Maybe her father's Florentine blue '42 Ford was driving there too, on a highway overhead. There was also a highway under her feet. If she just kept her hands on the steering wheel and looked at the road ahead.

The brick streets in Weatherford sounded like gravel on dirt road under her car.

83.

Flutie took geology field trips to Red Rock Canyon, the Wichita Mountains, Roman Nose. From Weatherford, they took Interstate 40, with its two highways on which traffic went its separate ways. The air sometimes brown with dirt.

Sometimes wildflowers bloomed, or a dead armadillo rocked on its back when a semi passed, its four feet in the air like cradle posts left by the road.

Flutie held a book of rocks open on her lap. Metamorphic. Sedimentary. Igneous.

Schist.

Selenite. The semi-transparent rock crystal from the Salt Plains. The name meant *stone of the moon.*

Ist ja gut, she thought.

Flutie read the history of the land, the story of the earth, the explanations of the rocks. How the land got to be how it was.

84.

Flutie went back to Vini for the weekend. At the Juke Box Blues in Woodward, Franklin's friends had something for her.

"I don't do that anymore." Flutie ran from the bar, the wind shoving itself in her face, blowing everything away except for the rocks.

85.

He wasn't a mechanic, or a cowboy, the second man who took Flutie to Texas. He was the instructor of her geology lab. She was going to the Palo Duro Canyon in Texas, south of Amarillo, in a van marked *Southwestern Oklahoma State University*, battered by

the wind crosswise on Interstate 40. Six students and
the lab instructor would study the white yokes of
shale in the red sandstone formation sometimes called
Spanish skirts. Flutie opened the window. The girl
behind her asked her to close it, and she did.

Flutie watched the fields flying by. She felt she
was going somewhere in the milky waves that washed
up from the old sea.

But where could she go? Where had Philomela
and Procne gone when they turned into a nightingale and a swallow? Had they remained birds,
flying around, doing what birds did? Or had they
turned back into women? Gone to college. Worked
at Carpter's Drygoods. Had the story gone on?

That's what was wrong with stories. They only
told a part. She had to listen, and later think about
the story, and fill in the rest. She had to interpret. To
decide where the story went.

86.

Digging in the red rock of Palo Duro Canyon,
Flutie heard the old voices of the land.

She thought of wind erosion and spatial pat-
terning. She thought of ocean basins and moving

plates of the earth. She thought of mapping. But mostly she thought of the land formations.

Flutie would study geology like she planned. Her focus would be the Salt Plains. Or maybe volcanoes. The reckless places of the earth. Even if they weren't in Oklahoma, she could know them just the same.

87.

Now Flutie was on the way back to Weatherford from the Palo Duro Canyon.

She saw a custom car pass on Interstate 40 from the other way. She turned and watched it go down the highway.

She moved her mouth as though she were talking. She saw the girl next to her watching. Flutie sat up and looked out the window of the van. She felt a red sandstone rock in her pocket. When she got back, she'd wrap it with string.

She remembered that she could talk. She remembered she was beginning to talk. She remembered she could hardly talk. She was still scared when she was in front of a class. She was still awkward. But she was beginning to feel what she could do.

Flutie decided she would teach. She would go back to Vini and teach all the students who couldn't talk. Especially if they'd been sealed up. Those who'd heard the voices of the town. The voices from deep in the earth. She'd place them in front of the class like candles that could not be blown out by the western Oklahoma wind.

COLOPHON

The text was set in Caslon, a type-
face designed by William Caslon I
(1692-1766). This face designed in
1725 has gone through many incar-
nations. It was the mainstay of
British printers for over one hundred years and remains very popular
today. The version use here is
Adobe Caslon. The display faces are
Insignia and Staccato 222.

Composed by Alabama Book
Composition, Deatsville, Alabama.

The book was printed by
R.R. Donnelley, Crawfordsville,
Indiana on acid free paper.